MAN WITH A MISSION

The sheriff puffed out his chest. It was time to get tough with this ruffian bounty hunter. Let him know this was *his* town.

"Now look here, mister . . ."

The bounty hunter stared hard at the elderly lawman, silencing him.

"No, *you* look here. Your town's no different than a hundred others I've been through. You and your citizens don't care if there's wanted men walking the streets as long as they're spending their money, and you don't care where they got it, as long as they leave most of it here when they ride out.

"Now I've got four hundred miles and ten days invested in those men, and that's enough. We're gonna end it today, one way or the other. And since you don't seem inclined to help, I suggest you stay out of my way."

Shaken, the sheriff asked, "Just who the hell you think you are, mister?"

Turning away, the man answered, "John Thomas Law, an' this just might be a good day for you to go fishin', Sheriff."

TEXAS TRACKER

SHOOT-OUT AT CORPUS CHRISTI

TOM CALHOUN

This is a work of fiction. Names, characters, places, and incidents either are the product of the author's imagination or are used fictitiously, and any resemblance to actual persons, living or dead, business establishments, events, or locales is entirely coincidental.

SHOOT-OUT AT CORPUS CHRISTI

A Jove Book / published by arrangement with
the author

PRINTING HISTORY
Jove edition / May 2002

Cover design by Steve Ferlauto.

For information address: The Berkley Publishing Group,
a division of Penguin Putnam Inc.,
375 Hudson Street, New York, New York 10014.

Visit our website at
www.penguinputnam.com

ISBN: 0-515-13294-2

A JOVE BOOK®
Jove Books are published by The Berkley Publishing Group,
a division of Penguin Putnam Inc.,
375 Hudson Street, New York, New York 10014.
JOVE and the "J" design
are trademarks belonging to Penguin Putnam Inc.

PRINTED IN THE UNITED STATES OF AMERICA

10 9 8 7 6 5 4 3 2 1

ONE

"THROW YOUR HANDS high, ya sonsabitches!"

The startled patrons of the Colfax Bank turned to find guns leveled at them by three men dressed in long black dusters. Kerchiefs concealed their identities.

"Anybody makes a fuss we'll kill the damn lot o' ya. That understood?"

The gruff-talking leader didn't need to repeat his threat as the patrons, their hands still held high, nodded that they fully understood the warning.

Motioning toward the teller's cage, the leader barked out, "Get them bags loaded up, boys, and make it quick."

The teller, a young man in his early twenties, was visibly shaking as the two men came behind the counter. His young eyes were fixed on the two guns pointed at him. Grabbing the boy by the collar, one of the bandits threw him aside and began grabbing up money from the cash drawer. No sooner had the teller slammed into the back wall than the other bank robber snatched him by the back of the neck and forced him to his knees in front of the safe.

"Now open it, boy. An' be damn quick about it!"

For a fleeting second the teller thought of telling them he didn't have the combination, but with the tone of their voices and the devil's glare in the eyes of the man standing over him, that was all it was, a fleeting thought. Some of the money in that safe belonged to him too, but it sure as hell wasn't enough to take a bullet in the head for. Spinning the dial right, then left, then back right, he felt the tumblers fall into place. Pushing the handle down, he swung the door open wide. Lifting his head as if in search of some sign of approval from the outlaw, the boy received the length of the man's gun barrel to the right side of his head for his trouble. The boy dropped like a rock, unconscious. Pushing the body aside with the toe of his boot, the outlaw knelt down and quickly filled the bag he was carrying.

"Gawdalmighty, boys! My ol' granny coulda robbed this damn place by now. Hurry it along!" shouted the leader.

Checking to make sure they had every dollar they could find, the two men swung themselves over the railing that separated the lobby from the cashier's cage. As one of the men's boots hit the floor on the other side, his kerchief suddenly slipped from his face. In a panic, he dropped his bag of money as he tried to pull the cloth back up and over his face, but it was too late. One of the men standing against the wall with his hands raised blurted out, "I'll be damned! It's Charlie Baxter."

Shaking his head from side to side and pulling his own mask down, the leader of the group, Nate Baxter, said, "Dammit, Charlie! No need to keep our faces covered now, boys. I'll hold these fellas till ya get mounted. Give a holler when yer ready to ride."

Grabbing up the dropped money bag, Charlie and Tom Baxter went out the door to where their younger brother, Coe Baxter, was holding the horses. Taking his reins from the boy, Charlie swung up in the saddle. Pulling his Colt .44, he shouted, "Get mounted, kid. Nate's about to bust this here town wide open."

Once all three were ready to ride, Tom yelled into the bank.

"Yo, Nate! Let's ride!"

Nate backed toward the door, keeping his gun leveled at the people against the wall. He paused in the doorway, and his eyes went to the man who had called out Charlie's name. Judging by his overalls, the man was a farmer.

"Ya know who I am, mister?"

Shifting nervously against the wall, the man replied, "Yes, sir. You're Nate Baxter."

A strange grin came over Nate's face.

"That's good. That's real good, farmer. Always figured when a man met his Maker he oughta be able to tell the Good Lord the name of the man that killed him."

In the blink of an eye Nate Baxter's Colt .45 roared. The bullet hit the surprised farmer in the chest, driving him back against the wall and splattering those around him with blood. The man was dead before he hit the floor.

Smiling at the others, Nate said, "Just goes to show ya. Sometimes a fella can know too much."

The gunshot had drawn the attention of people on the street who, until then, had had no idea what was going on. Still not sure, a number of them started toward the bank. Suddenly they saw a man bolt through the doorway and join three other men in front of the bank who were mounted and had their guns drawn. Any further confusion suddenly vanished as one of the people inside yelled, "Help! Help! They're robbin' the bank! Get your guns, boys!"

But it was already too late. Whipping their horses at a full gallop, the Baxter brothers were already at the far end of the street. Hearing the gunshot and the commotion, the sheriff opened his office door and stepped out, just in time to be met with a hail of gunfire from the outlaws as they rode past. He was hit more than seven times, and there was little doubt the man was dead.

As the dust settled over the main street of Colfax, Texas, the people found themselves with an empty bank vault, two dead bodies, and the dubious honor of being the first town to fall victim to the Baxter brothers, whose rampage across Texas was just beginning.

Two weeks after the Colfax robbery, the brothers struck again. This time in the town of Fredricksburg. There they robbed the bank, killing the bank manager and a teller. Four days later they hit the Austin-to-Waco stage, killing the driver, the shotgun rider, and a woman passenger, but not before Nate and Charlie had their way with her.

Their reputation as ruthless and dangerous men was spreading quickly across the state, but it wasn't until they ambushed and killed two Texas Rangers that the public began to realize just how cold-blooded and dangerous these men really were. In the town of Nacogdoches the outlaws used one of Tom's whores from Mattie's to lure the two unsuspecting lawmen into a vacant lot. While the Rangers were talking to the girl, the brothers, hiding in ambush, opened fire on the trio with ten-gauge shotguns. The girl was killed instantly, and both Rangers went down badly wounded. Tossing the shotguns aside, the brothers then encircled the two helpless lawmen and shot them to pieces with their six-guns. It was Nate Baxter's way of sending a message to the best lawmen in the state: *Your Ranger reputation don't mean a damn thing to us!*

While the Baxters were counting their money and planning the next robbery, a hundred miles to the west another dangerous man was making plans of his own.

John Taylor Law hooked his right leg over the saddlehorn and took out the makings to roll himself a cigarette. Striking a match on the horn, he cupped the flame in his hand and lit up. He inhaled deeply, letting the smoke curl slowly out of the corner of his mouth. As he did, the big buckskin he rode shifted his weight, first to the left, then back to the right. Reaching forward, his rider gently rubbed his neck.

"Okay, Toby. I know you're tired, fella. We both are. But we're almost there. We hit town, I'll see you get a rubdown and double feed, okay? What'd you think of that?"

The buckskin raised his head, shook his mane, and whinnied as if signaling his approval. It was a sign of a longtime relationship between horse and rider.

Tossing the smoke aside, the big man in the long, black frock coat pulled his Colt .45 from the tied-down holster and checked its load. Satisfied, he twirled the perfectly balanced Peacemaker one time, then slid it back into place on his hip. Next, he pushed back the left side of the coat and removed a second Colt .45 from a shoulder rig. This one was a short-barrel model. Checking the chambers, he slipped the preferred weapon of most gunfighters back into the rig. Toby snorted a couple of times to show his growing impatience with his master.

"Okay, Toby. Reckon we're as ready as we'll ever be."

Dropping the right leg to the side and booting the stirrup, J.T. gave Toby a gentle nudge and the two moved on past a fading wooden sign that read, SHERMAN, TEXAS, 2 MILES.

The sheriff in Sherman was a man named Jake Potter. He was in his mid-to-late fifties, with graying hair and a gut that hung over a sagging gunbelt. Sitting in his favorite chair outside his office, he was busy whittling on a block of wood when he first saw the buckskin and its rider appear at the far end of the street. Normally he wouldn't give such a sight a second thought. Sherman was located in north Texas, not far from the southernmost boundaries of Indian Territory or the Nations, as some folks called it. It wasn't unusual to have a considerable number of strangers passing through his town on a daily basis. But there was something about this lone rider that already had the old lawman nervous. He couldn't explain it, but there it was. Shifting his attention back to his block of wood, Potter laughed to himself. He was sure going jumpy in his old age. With any luck at all this stranger would walk that big buckskin right by him and right on out of town. But this wasn't to be Jake Potter's lucky day.

Wheeling Toby to the right and stopping directly in front of the sheriff, J.T. rested his arm across the saddle-horn and leaned forward, waiting for the lawman to look up. Potter had hoped to ignore the man as he rode past, but now that wasn't possible. Raising his head, Potter looked up at the big man, his lawman instincts taking in every detail within a matter of seconds. Black Stetson hat, good-quality frock coat that fitted well across broad shoulders. White shirt, black string tie with gold oval slide. Black vest with silver buttons. A gold chain trailed to the watch pocket of the vest. The rest of the outfit was of equally good quality. Black pants covered the tops of expensive but well-worn boots that would cost the average cowpuncher three months pay. Everything was covered in trail dust. The stranger had traveled a lot of miles.

Taking in the face, Potter figured the man to be in his mid-to-late thirties. It was hard to tell with the dust and at least a week's growth of beard covering the face. The hair was black and hadn't been cut in a while. Piercing blue-green eyes and a square-set jaw gave the face a look of strong character. Taking into account the long legs and broad shoulders, Potter figured the man to be just a little over six feet with the proper amount of muscle and weight to fit the frame. The old lawman might be a little long in the tooth, but he could still size up a man better than most, and he'd just done a hell of a job sizing up John Thomas Law.

Tossing the splinter of wood he had left to the side, Potter smiled and in a friendly tone asked, "Somethin' I can do for you, mister?"

J.T. shifted in the saddle. "That'll be your choice, Sheriff."

Potter stood up. Brushing the shavings from his clothes, he looked a little confused by the man's answer. "Come again? Don't think I get your meanin', mister."

J.T. pulled two folded pieces of paper from inside his coat. Leaning forward, he passed them to Potter.

"I'm after those two men and I have good reason to believe they're here in your town."

Potter unfolded the paper and found himself staring at two wanted posters. One was a man named Zeb Wilson, who was charged with three counts of murder, and the other was called Gabe Cross, wanted for murder, rape, and stage robbery. The old lawman studied the two posters with the rough drawings and general descriptions, but nothing about either man seemed familiar.

" 'Fraid I can't help you none, mister. We get a lot of folks through here every day. Only ones I take notice of are them that cause me trouble. You the law?"

"Not exactly," came the reply.

Folding the papers again, Potter passed them back to the stranger. The smile and friendly tone of earlier were suddenly gone as the lawman said, "Well, then. If you ain't the law, I take it you're a bounty hunter. That right?"

Returning the papers to his coat pocket, J.T. nodded. "That's right, Sheriff. You got a problem with that?"

"Nope. But there might be a few folks round here figure you fellas in that business deal in blood money. But I got no problem with it myself. Why you figure those two boys are in my town?"

"Been trackin' 'em ten days now. Thought I might catch up with 'em this mornin' an brace 'em at their camp. Figure I missed 'em by an hour. Tracks led straight to Sherman. They're here, all right. Now whether you help me with the arrest or not is up to you. But either way, I'm going to find them before I leave here."

Jake Potter had been sheriff for five years, and had just been reelected to another term. He'd survived being a lawman in this part of the country by staying clear of men like Wilson and Cross. Okay, so they were wanted men. They hadn't committed any crimes in his town, and as long as they didn't he had no problem with leaving them to go about their drinking and whoring uninterrupted. In a few days they'd get bored and move on anyway. Seemed like good solid reasoning to him. The town made money, he didn't get shot full of holes, and the men left town feeling they'd had a good time. What was wrong with that? Now this bounty man rides in here and wants to upset the whole scheme of things. Just who the hell did he think he was anyhow?

Puffing out his chest, while at the same time trying to pull up his gunbelt, Potter figured it was time to get tough with this damn bounty hunter and make it clear that this was Jake Potter's town.

"Now you look here, mister! You go startin' any trouble in my town and you're liable to find yourself behind some damn bars. You wanta deal with them boys, then you do it outside of my town. I don't want folks thinkin' I deal with bounty hunters. That could be downright unhealthy for this town and me both. That plain enough talk for you?"

J.T. stared long and hard at the lawman, then nodded. "Oh, it's plain enough all right, Sheriff. This town ain't no different than all the others I've be in. You and your damn good citizens don't mind wanted men walkin' the streets as long as they keep it tame and spread their money around. Nobody wants to hear how or where they got that money just as long as they leave most of it here. An' you got the nerve to talk to me about blood money. Hell, compared to you damn bunch of sanctimonious hypocrites, I'm a goddamn saint."

Potter pointed his finger at J.T. "Now you look here, mister. We—"

The bounty hunter cut him off before he could finish.

"No! You look here! I've got four hundred miles and ten days invested in those two men, and I don't have any intention of spending one more day or going one more mile chasin' after 'em. We're gonna end this game today, one way or another. You've made your point clear enough, Sheriff. Now I'm makin' mine. Since you don't seem inclined to help, I suggest you stay the hell out of my way. That plain enough talk for you, Sheriff?"

Clearly shaken by this sudden verbal attack, Potter asked, "Just who the hell are you, mister?"

Pulling rein, the bounty man began to back the buckskin away from the hitch rail as he answered, "John Thomas Law, an' this might be a good day for you to go fishin', lawman."

Having had his say, J.T. headed down the main street for the stables, leaving a stunned Jake Potter meekly returning to his chair. All the color seemed to have drained from the old lawman's face on hearing the man's name. Watching the horse and rider disappear into the barn, Potter muttered to himself, "J.T. Law. I'll be damned. Them boys Wilson and Cross are good as dead already."

Bob Irwin, owner of the local barbershop, came strolling down the boardwalk. Seeing Potter in his chair, he remarked, "Gonna be a nice day today, Jake."

The sheriff nodded. "Sure enough, Bob. Damn good day to go fishin'."

J.T.'S REASON FOR going to the stables was twofold. One, to get Toby taken care of, and two, to search for two specific horses. He spotted Zeb Wilson's Appaloosa as soon as he entered the barn. But a search of the other stalls failed to locate the chestnut roan belonging to Gabe Cross. The two men had been riding together for the last ten days and J.T. had followed the same two sets of prints into town. Maybe Cross had decided it was time for them to split up. A man on the run developed a strange sort of sixth sense about such things. J.T. Law could attest to that from personal experience. Maybe that sixth sense had told Cross it wasn't safe to lay over in Sherman.

The bounty hunter's concerns were quickly put to rest when the stable boy told him they had been unusually busy the last few days and had had to keep some of the horses in a special pen out back of the barn. Tipping the boy two bits, J.T. walked out to the special corral. There among three other horses stood a big chestnut roan. Opening the gate, J.T. walked slowly over to the well-built animal and began stroking the horse's neck to calm him, then bent down and pulled the right foot up to check the shoe. He found what he was looking for—a small V-shaped nick in the metal of the shoe. Five days into the chase, J.T. had noticed the change in the print. It had appeared the same day the two men had crossed a section of the Texas Pacific Railroad. The roan's huff had come down at an awkward angle on an offset railway spike, causing a slight indentation in the shoe. This horse belonged to Gabe Cross, no doubt about it.

On his way out of the barn, J.T. inquired as to how long the owners of those two horses had planned to keep them there. The boy told him he was to have them ready to go first thing the following morning.

Tossing his saddlebags over his shoulder, J.T. walked a short distance back up the street to the hotel. While the clerk got his key, he scanned the register. There was no Wilson or Cross listed on the book. But then, he hadn't expected to find them there. Neither man would be using his real name.

The room had the basics. A worn-out bed with a small table and kerosene lamp beside it. A four-drawer dresser and another small table that held a washbasin and a pitcher of water. Above that hung a broken mirror. The room had a musty smell to it, with a strong hint of urine from when cowboys had missed the chamber pot or hadn't bothered to use it at all. Tossing his saddlebags onto the bed, he opened the windows to let some fresh air into the room. The broken-down mattress sagged under his weight as he sat down and rolled himself a cigarette.

Slowly blowing the smoke across the room, J.T. pondered his next move. Wilson and Cross were apparently not planning to leave until morning. That meant he would have time for a long-overdue bath, a hot meal of steak and taters, and a chance to catch up on some much-needed sleep. God knows he was tired. These two boys had given him a run for the money, but that was all over now. He had them right where he wanted them. The idea of a hot bath and some sleep sounded pretty good. But then a thought crossed his mind. What if Wilson and Cross changed their minds? What if they suddenly just decided to pack it in and ride out later in the afternoon? That would be two thousand dollars that rode out of town while he was sleeping. No. He'd been after these boys for a long time. No matter how tired he was, it was best to take care of business first. He could relax later.

Flipping the remains of the cigarette out the window, J.T. took his room key off the nightstand and shoved it into his pocket. Brushing most of the trail dust off his coat, he went downstairs and stood in front of the hotel. There were over twenty saloons in Sherman, and it was a good bet that he'd find the men he was looking for in one of them. As he started to cross the street he saw Sheriff Potter riding his way. As the two men stared long and hard at one another, someone shouted from the boardwalk.

"Hey, Jake! Where ya off to?"

Without taking his eyes off the bounty man, the sheriff replied, "Gotta go identify a prisoner over in Dennison. Won't be back till tomorrow night."

J.T. nodded his approval as the old lawman rode by. Jake Potter had a strong sense of self-preservation. He'd decided the best way to play out this hand was by not becoming involved at all in the situation. He couldn't be held responsible for anything that happened while he was out of town.

J.T. had been to six saloons by the time he entered the Ambrose. He had only gone a few feet inside when he spotted his prey. Gabe Cross was standing at the far end of the bar pouring himself a drink from a whiskey bottle. Zeb Wilson sat at a poker table only a few feet away and to the right of the bar. He was involved in a card game with three cowboys and had never taken notice of the big man in black as he entered the bar. Cross, on the other hand, hadn't taken his eyes off J.T. since the big man had walked through the doors. He studied J.T. long and hard as he poured himself another drink.

Gabe Cross was supposedly the faster of the two. He wore a Colt .45 hitched high with no tie-down and the holster titled slightly back and to the rear. The sign of a man who practiced a lot and knew exactly where his gun had to be positioned for maximum speed. Zeb Wilson carried a Colt .44 and wore his holster low to give himself more room for the long barrel to clear the top of the leather. Wilson was more the typical bushwhacker and backshooter rather than a gunman. It was Gabe Cross who was the true threat.

"Gawdammit all to hell! That's four hands in a row I lost to you damn cowboys. I didn't know no better, I'd swear you boys was cheatin' hell outta me."

A sudden silence came over the room. There weren't that many people in the place, but when they heard the word "cheatin'," all eyes focused on the poker table.

Racking in the poker chips from the last hand, the youngest of the drovers, a kid who looked barely more than seventeen, laughed as he said, "Hell, mister. Ain't noboby gotta cheat you. You're the worst damn poker player I ever set a table with. Raisin' that pot on a pair of half-assed deuces. What the hell was you thinking?"

From the bar, J.T. saw Wilson's hand move casually down to his .44. Wilson was going to kill the cowboy for what he'd just said. Gabe Cross must have realized that too. He turned toward the table ready to back Wilson's play. Their was little doubt in J.T.'s mind that the outlaws would kill all three of the unsuspecting cowboys before the young drovers even had an idea what was going on. Just as Wilson was about to pull his gun, J.T. stepped out away from the bar and yelled out, "Zeb Wilson!"

His gun already halfway out of the holster, Wilson paused and looked toward the end of the bar and the man who had just called out his name. He saw a big man dressed in black with his feet slightly apart who was pushing the right side of his coat back behind his gunbelt. Shifting slightly in his chair to hide his gun hand from the man at the bar, Wilson asked, "Do I know you, mister?"

Gabe Cross had now turned away from the cowboys and was focusing all his attention on the man in black.

Ignoring Wilson's question, J.T. told the three cowboys to get up slowly from the table and to keep their hands where he could see them. The drovers didn't hesitate. Slowly sliding their chairs back, and being extra careful to keep their hands away from their gunbelts, they moved back against the wall, holding their hands out in front of them at all times.

Still sitting at the table, Wilson had his gun hand out of sight. Slowly he eased his thumb up and cocked the Colt .44 as he asked, "You a lawman, mister?"

"Hell, no, he ain't no goddamn lawman," shouted Gabe Cross in a booming voice. "He's a damn bounty man. I thought I recognized you when you came in here, but I wasn't sure. Zeb, this here fella is J.T. Law. I told you the other night I felt like somebody was doggin' us. Well, this here is the top dog in the business. Ain't that right, John Thomas?"

Zeb Wilson's thumb was frozen on the hammer of his Colt. This was the man who had every outlaw in the state of Texas looking over his shoulder, expecting him to appear out of nowhere, as J.T. Law often did with most of his victims. They said he'd killed fourteen men, and that was just the ones folks knew about. Now, here he stood as big as life and he was all business.

J.T. stood perfectly still, his right hand hanging loose and relaxed next to his .45.

"Okay, boys. You know why I'm here. You both got paper out on you and I mean to collect. We can do this nice and easy or the hard way. Choice is yours. But either way we're goin' out together. You call it."

A broad smile suddenly broke across Gabe Cross's face.

"I'll be damned! Folks said you was a polite sonofabitch. Reckon they was right. But seein' as how they're gonna hang me anyhow, I think I'd like to try my luck."

J.T. could respect that. Hanging was a terrible way to die. He nodded.

"Thought you might feel that way, Gabe. I'll give you the first move. Go when you're ready."

Zeb Wilson was about to piss his pants. The last thing he wanted to do was match guns with J.T. Law. He was about to say just that when Gabe Cross went for his gun. The saloon exploded in gunfire. The sound was almost deafening. Gabe Cross had drawn first, but before he could get off a single shot, J.T. had already put two holes in him. Clutching his chest with one hand, Cross tried to raise his gun, but it was no use. His shot went into the floor a few feet in front of him and he fell to the floor. He was dead.

At the sound of the first shot, Zeb Wilson leaped out of his chair to get out of the way. His mistake was coming out of the chair with his gun in his hand. Whether he meant to fire or not didn't matter. The sight of the .44 was enough for J.T., who fired twice, hitting the bad poker player once in the chest and once in the throat. Zeb had a shocked look on his face as he tried to say something, but only blood came out of his mouth. His eyes rolled back and he fell over the card table dead.

Dropping the four spent bullets out of his gun and replacing them, J.T. holstered the weapon and walked out of the saloon. He passed a rush of curious onlookers and went back to his hotel. He hadn't been in his room more than a few minutes when there was a knock on his door. Pulling the short Colt from the shoulder rig, he cocked it and holding it behind his back, slowly opened the door.

The visitor was a tall, skinny fellow named Felix Crump, Potter's deputy. He held an envelope in one hand and legal papers in the other. He'd made a point of not wearing his gun and he was shaking like a leaf. His first attempt to speak produced lip movement but no words. Finally, he managed to say, "Sheriff signed these 'fore he left. Said I was to bring 'em to your room after your meetin' with them two boys was over."

Holding out his right hand, the deputy continued. "Money's in this here envelope, but I'll need ya to sign these here papers 'fore I can give it to ya. That is, if that's all right, Mr. Law."

J.T. couldn't help but grin. Ol' Man Potter wanted him long gone by the time he got back from Dennison. By doing all the paperwork before he left, he had saved J.T. at least a three-day wait. Inviting the man in, J.T. signed all the legal forms and counted the money in the envelope. Everything was in perfect order.

"Your sheriff seems to have been pretty confident that I could handle these two men. Wonder what he'd done if I'd lost. Guess he didn't plan on that."

Now Felix was grinning. "Oh, yes, sir, he did. Said if you was killed I was to spread all this here money round the bars for free drinks to everybody that came in. Would've been a hell of a party too."

Suddenly realizing what he'd just said, Felix's face went white. "I . . . I didn't mean . . . uh, I didn't mean I was looking forward to you dyin', Mr. Law. I . . . I just meant."

J.T. took five dollars from the stack of bills, shoved it into the deputy's shirt pocket, and with a smile said, "Hey, relax, Felix. Go have yourself a few drinks on me." Peeling off another five, he shoved it in the pocket. "An' give that to your boss when he gets back. Tell him it's his share of the blood money."

Looking confused, but eager to get out of the room, Felix thanked J.T. and took off down the hall. J.T. had just poured himself a drink when there was another knock at the door. The visitor this time was Billy Tyler, a Texas Ranger. He had been sent out to find J.T. at the request of Abe Covington, captain of Rangers out of Austin. He was asking J.T. to come to Austin as a personal favor. He was having a problem with a bunch called the Baxter brothers and he figured John Thomas Law was just the man to handle that problem for him.

TWO

★

THE RIDE TO Austin was a long and dusty one, but one that J.T. found almost downright pleasurable thanks to the company of Billy Tyler. The young Texas Ranger possessed a vast knowledge of frontier skills and experience that far exceeded his youthful appearance. He enjoyed the respect of his fellow Rangers, nearly all of whom were twice his age. Billy had earned that respect through his demonstrations of courage and bravery on a number of occasions in running gun battles with Comanches, outlaws, and Mexican bandits. An excellent horseman, the boy was as quick of wit as he was with his gun—a quality J.T. found admirable given the near-impossible job of the Texas Rangers.

This small group of dedicated men was tasked with the responsibility of trying to bring law and order to the farthest regions of this harsh and unforgiving land called Texas, which was larger than some countries. Billy Tyler was nineteen and he was a Texas Ranger.

As the two men approached the outskirts of Austin, Billy leaned down out of the saddle, plucked a piece of prairie grass, sat upright again, and placed the tip of the grass in the corner of his mouth.

"J.T., how come ya don't join up with us? Cap'in's got two companies short on men right now. I know he'd put one of them Ranger badges on ya faster'n snot on a cold-ass day."

J.T. couldn't help but laugh. Smiling over at his young companion, he shook his head. "Damn, Billy. Where do you come up with those expressions of yours?"

With the prairie grass still hanging from the corner of his mouth, and a smile that went from ear to ear on that young face, he replied, "Don't rightly know, J.T., they just sorta come to me, ya know. The cap'in says I got a u . . . uni . . . uh . . ."

The boy paused a moment as if in deep thought. Then his face lit up again as he continued. "Unique! That's it! The cap'in says I got a unique way of expressin' myself."

J.T. laughed again. "Can't argue with that."

"So how come, J.T.?"

"How come what?"

"How come ya ain't a Texas Ranger? I mean, ya just took down two outlaws back there in Sherman single-handed, but I swear them townspeople didn't seem all that appreciative of what ya'd done. But now, if ya'd been wearin' a badge, they'd 'a been pumpin' your hand and slappin' ya on the back, tellin' ya what a great job ya was doin' for the people and the great state of Texas. All I'm sayin' is, them two fellows was wanted men, all right, but a badge seems to make it more legal, I guess. Ya know what I'm sayin'?"

The smile was gone from J.T.'s face. But it wasn't because he was upset with Billy. Hell, the kid had asked a fair enough question.

"That's right Billy. Cross and Wilson were both wanted men with a price on their heads. A price put there by those same self-righteous citizens that do all the back-slappin' and hand-pumpin' 'cause you're wearin' a badge. Hell, Billy, they don't give a damn who laid them boys low, just as long as none of them had to do it. Gettin' it done by a man with a badge just makes it set a little easier on their minds, that's all. Then I show up and remind them that it was the good citizens that paid for the killing of those two men. That's what really bothers them. The idea that one man profits from the death of other men."

Billy rode along in silence for a while as he pondered the bounty hunter's answer.

"I suppose yer right, J.T., but all the same, people don't talk 'bout lawmen like they do 'bout you fellas. No, sir. I've heard you boys called some pretty sorry names, let me tell ya. An' trust me, there weren't a lick of respect in any of 'em."

Looking down at his badge and wiping the dust off, Billy continued. "Respect. That's what this here badge brings with it. Don't ya figure yer owed a little respect for what ya do, J.T.? I mean, it just ain't anybody could go up against men like Cross and Wilson, or the others ya faced. That outta be worth somethin'."

J.T. leaned out and spat before he answered. "They can keep their goddamn respect, Billy. Just be damn sure you've got my money when the job's done. We'll sort out the moral issues when we all meet in hell."

Billy laughed. "Oh. Come on now, J.T., tell me how ya really feel about it."

Both men were still laughing when they moved their horses up to the hitch rail in front of Ranger Headquarters. Captain Abe Covington was just coming out of his office as the two riders swung down out of the saddle.

"Ranger Tyler. Glad to see you found him so quick."

J.T. flipped the reins of the buckskin over the rail as he asked, "How's the Ranger business, Abe?"

"Not near as damn profitable as yours from what I hear. Got a message in on my desk from a sheriff up in Sherman. He don't seem to like you much. Says you gunned down Gabe Cross and Zeb Wilson. That right?"

Young Billy's eyes seemed to light up. "Sure enough, Cap'in. Saw 'em all laid out in the undertaker's myself. Two shots each. At two hundred fifty dollars a shot, that ain't bad wages."

The excitement in the boy's voice wasn't lost on the captain, who was now frowning at him. "You sayin' you're not happy with a lawman's pay, Ranger Tyler?"

Caught off guard by the captain's hard look and sudden change of tone, Billy was stammering for a reply.

"Guess you figure you're fast enough with that popper of yours to be a bounty hunter like Mr. Law here," said Covington. "That right?"

"No . . . no, sir. Didn't mean nothing like that. Not a'tall."

"Glad to hear that. The boys are out back gettin' ready to run the gauntlet. Why don't you join 'em?"

Avoiding his captain's stare, Billy replied, "Yes, sir." And led his horse away.

Like J.T., Abe Covington was a big man. He stood over six feet, with broad shoulders and a pair of arms that looked as if they could squeeze the life out of a grizzly bear. He had a heavy stock of chestnut hair, and dark brown eyes that always seemed to be studying the person he was talking to. A well-kept long mustache with its tips drooping just below the chin gave the Ranger a certain cavalier look. As they walked into the office, Covington motioned toward a chair in front of his desk.

"Set yourself, J.T. I'll pour us a drink. Figure you could use one after your long ride."

The Ranger didn't have to offer twice. Dropping down into the chair, J.T. replied, "That's sounds damn good to me."

Blowing the ever-constant dust from two glasses, Covington filled them to the top.

"I appreciate you coming, John Thomas. Wasn't sure where you were or what you were working when I sent Tyler out after you. But I figured if anyone could find you, he could."

Handing J.T. his glass of whiskey, the Ranger moved behind his desk and sat down. J.T. took a hefty drink. The stinging bite of the whiskey burnt his dry mouth, almost numbing it as it worked its magic, sending a warm feeling down his throat, then spreading that warmth through his tired, saddle-worn muscles.

"You know, Abe. That kid Tyler's got a lot of trail sense to be so young. You're lucky to have him."

Covington smiled. "You're right about that. He gets a mite cocky sometimes, so I have to take him down a peg or two just to remind him that he's still nineteen and don't know it all yet. But he can ride and shoot with the best of 'em. The boys all like him. Guess when you put a hat on it, he makes a hell of a fine Ranger."

J.T. nodded in agreement and took another shot of his whiskey. "Now tell me, Abe. Why'd you send for me? I know it wasn't to talk over old times."

Covington's face took on a serous look. Picking up a paper from his desk, he passed it over to J.T.

It was a telegram from the commanding officer at Fort Supply in Indian Territory. He reported that seventy-five to a hundred Comanches led by a young war chief called Iron Hand had jumped the reservation and were believed to have crossed the Red River into Texas. They were well armed and spoiling for a fight. Washington had already been notified of the breakout and the commander was awaiting instructions. He advised that all towns, farms, and ranches in north Texas be alerted as soon as possible. According to the date, the telegram was two days old.

J.T. placed the paper back on the desk. "I suppose you've already warned the folks along the Red about this."

Covington leaned back in his chair, rolling the glass of whiskey back and forth between the palms of his hands. "Sent telegrams off to the towns I could, and riders to most of the others. But we're already getting back reports of burnt-out farms and ranches. So far this Iron Hand and his war party have killed at least sixteen people, an' that's just the ones we know about."

J.T. stared at the huge map of Texas that hung on the wall to the side of the captain's desk. "Been a long time since we had any Indian trouble."

Covington turned in his chair and stared up at the map as well. "Yeah, but it don't really surprise me none. Ever since Custer and the Seventh were wiped out last summer, the word spread among the tribes that if the Sioux could defeat the white man, then maybe they could too. I'm just surprised its took this long for someone to jump the reservation."

"So you figure this Iron Hand has convinced a few of his boys that they can do the same as the Sioux by raising a little hell down here in Texas."

"That's about it. If he can pull it off, the young upstart hopes to spark a full-scale uprisin' among all the tribes in the Nations. That's why it's so damn important that we round them up as quick as we can. Stop any others from getting any ideas about joinin' up with him."

J.T. finished his whiskey and set the glass on the desk in front of him. "Okay, Abe. So you got an Indian problem, but I don't think that's why you sent for me. Tyler mentioned the Baxter brothers, but that was about it. Said you'd give me the details when we got here. I take it they're the reason I'm here."

Covington poured himself another drink, then pushed the bottle over toward the bounty man.

"No, thanks, Abe. I better hold off till I've had a chance to get something to eat."

Leaning back in his chair, Covington took a long pull on the whiskey and shook his head. "Bad bunch, J.T. Shoot people just for the pure hell of it. Robbed two banks and a stage. Couple of 'em raped a woman passenger, then killed her stone-cold dead. Takin' a life don't mean a thing to these boys. Just as soon kill you as look at you."

The Ranger captain paused a moment. J.T. could clearly see a look of sadness suddenly appear in the lawman's eyes as he waited for him to continue. When he did, that same sadness was in his voice.

"They bushwhacked two of my Rangers. Marv Longley and Ben Crowder. After the stage robbery, the Baxters left a trail clear enough for a one-eyed drunk to follow. Lead my boys straight to Nacogdoches. They hadn't been in town an hour when a young gal from one of the saloons came to see them. Said she could lead 'em to where the Baxters were hidin'. Said they was all whiskeyed up and passed out."

J.T. shook his head slowly from side to side. He didn't know Ben Crowder, but he had played a few cards and shared a drink or two with Ol' Marv Longley on those occasions when their trails crossed. The old Ranger had been in his mid-fifties and had counted J.T. as a friend.

"Can't believe Ol' Marv wouldn't see through that as some kind of setup," said J.T.

Covington readily agreed. "That troubled me too when I first heard what happened. Marv hadn't survived all those years by bein' a horse's ass. The Baxters paid that gal to go to the Rangers, and just to make it look good, they beat hell out of her first. They paid her extra for that. She told Marv she was turnin' them boys in for what they'd done to her. Figure Marv took one look at the gal's face and saw plenty of reason for her to feel that way."

That made sense to J.T. "So she leads them right into it then?"

"Sure enough. From what we could find out, she took the boys to a vacant lot down by the stockyards. The Baxters were waitin' with scatterguns. Once she got 'em in the center of the lot, the Baxters cut loose on 'em."

J.T.'s eyebrows rose as he asked, "The girl too?"

"Damn straight. Nearly cut that girl in half with them shotguns. Both Marv and Ben went down before they had a chance to draw their guns. Ben was killed outright, but Ol' Marv was still alive when they came outta hidin' and formed a circle around him. Folks say they laughed at him, then drew their guns an' shot him to pieces. His own mother wouldn't have recognized him when it was over."

"An' you're certain it was the Baxters that did this?"

Covington nodded. "Hell, the damn cowards didn't even try to hide it. They went through every saloon in town braggin' how they'd sent two Rangers to hell and had more of the same waitin' for anyone else that got in their way. Like I said, J.T., they're a damn mean bunch."

The image of Marv Longley lying in the dirt, wounded and withering in pain from a shotgun blast, surrounded by a group of laughing bastards who then shot him to pieces a little at a time, sent a fire rushing through the bounty man's veins.

"So when you going after these sonsabitches?" he asked.

Covington shook his head. "We're can't."

J.T. leaned forward in his chair. There was fire in his eyes now. "What d'you mean, you can't?"

Covington came out of his chair and tapped the map with a finger as he said, "J.T., I got sixteen dead Texas citizens along the Red and near onto a hundred Comanches runnin' wild somewhere over an area six hundred miles long. It's gonna take every Ranger we got in Texas an' plenty of troops to track 'em down. I got no time or people to be goin' out after the Baxters right now. That's why I sent for you. I need someone who can deal with these bastards on their own terms. You want the job?"

J.T.'s eyes roamed over the map. Covington was right. Finding the Comanches would be like looking for a needle in a haystack. He didn't doubt they'd find Iron Hand, but it was going to take time. Meanwhile, that left the Baxters free to rape, rob, and murder whenever or wherever they pleased. From what he'd heard, J.T. was convinced that if ever a bunch needed to be looking at a short rope with a long drop, it was the Baxters. He'd already made up his mind that he was going after them for what they'd done to Marv Longley, but he was a businessman as well. Just as J.T. Law had a reputation as a persistent manhunter and deadly gunfighter, it was also well known that he did nothing for free.

"How much?" he asked.

Abe Covington had been waiting patiently for the man's answer.

"How much what?" asked Covington.

J.T. smiled. "Hell, Abe, you know I don't work for free. How much is the state of Texas willing to pay for my services to rid themselves of the Baxter brothers?"

J.T. watched a frown cut across the Ranger's face. Covington's dark eyes narrowed as he leaned forward with his hands on his hips.

"I'll be damned! Here I've told you what those bastards done and you ain't concerned about nothin' but goddamn money. I swear, man. Don't you have any sense of decency or right? Does everything have to come with a price fixed to it? Hell, you're a Texan. Why don't you do something for the people of Texas just once? Not for money, but because it's just the right thing to do."

J.T. was on his feet quick as a cat, a hard look on his face and fire in his eyes.

"Right, my ass! Was it right when they took my ranch while I was off fighting a damn war, Abe? They left me with nothin'. I came home and I didn't have two damn spoons to rub together or a pot to piss in! But anybody try to help me out? Hell, no, they didn't. I damn near starved to death that first month home. Goddamn lawyers were afraid to take on the carpetbaggers that stole it, and the tight-ass bankers wouldn't loan me a nickel to get started again. Then there were those damn Yankee troops of the occupation force givin' me shit everywhere I went all because I was a Johnny Reb. If I hadn't left for Kansas when I did, I swear I'd have ended up killin' some of those bastards and the good folks of Texas would've strung me from a cottonwood for havin' done it. So don't talk to me about goddamn right!"

Abe Covington wasn't backing off. "Yeah, but when you got back on your feet, where'd you end up, J.T.? Texas! That's where. You're a damn Texan clean down to your boots an' we both know it. But I swear, J.T., everything doesn't have to come with a price on it."

"The hell it don't!"

"You didn't charge me for saving my life in Fort Worth three years ago."

That statement gave J.T. cause to pause a moment. He remembered the occasion well. This tall Ranger had walked into the Acme Saloon bold as brass to arrest two men for stage robbery and murder. The entire place had gone quiet the moment they saw the badge. Everyone knew why the lawman was there, and the smart ones at the bar had slowly moved away, leaving only the two men he was after standing at the bar.

J.T. had been at a poker table at the time and watched the drama unfold. If Abe Covington was worried about the odds, he sure hadn't shown it that day. The Ranger told the two to drop their guns, they were under arrest. Of course they had no intention of going peaceably, and in the ensuing gunfight, Covington had killed both men in the blink of an eye. But as he knelt down to check on the two men, a third man stepped from behind a curtain with a ten-gauge shotgun, and would have blown the Ranger's head off if it hadn't been for J.T., who drew his Colt from his shoulder holster and dispatched the would-be backshooter with two well-placed shots, one in the chest and the other in the head. The affair had marked the beginning of a friendship that had lasted ever since.

Now, realizing that he was allowing bitter memories of the past to overrule common sense and endanger that friendship, J.T. relieved the tension of the moment.

"Yeah, now that you mention it, I been meanin' to send you a bill for that."

The two men stared across the desk at each other in silence for a moment. Try as he might, Covington couldn't keep a straight face, and a smile that started at the corner of his lip spread upward. Breaking out in a laugh, he said, "You're a real bastard, you know that, don't you?"

J.T. was smiling broadly as he replied, "Hell, yes, I am. I'm a Texan, remember. Now how much?"

"Thousand dollars apiece." said Covington, this time without a moment of hesitation. "There's no paper out on 'em yet, but I'm authorizing it. Have the warrants drawn up within the hour."

"That warrant going to state dead or alive?"

"That's right, J.T. Dead or alive. But I'm bettin' my

money on dead. Those boys ain't givin' themselves up to the law or anybody else. They done crossed the line an' bought into this game all the way when they killed those two Rangers, and they know it. They figure they got nothin' to lose now. You might wanta keep that in mind."

"Always do, Captain. Now, if that's all, I'd like to get a bath, something to eat, and a little sleep before I head out again."

Covington reached across the desk and extended his hand.

"Thanks, J.T."

The bounty man took the outstretched hand in a firm grip and as they shook, J.T. grinned. "You know I'd have done this for Ol' Marv anyway, don't you?"

Covington returned the smile. "Hell, I already figured that before you rode up here."

The two men left the office and walked outside. As J.T. was pulling the reins from the hitch rail, there came the sudden crack of gunshots mixed with cheers and laughter. It was coming from behind the headquarters building. J.T.'s first reaction was to reach for his Colt, but Covington quickly raised his hands and shook his head.

"It's okay, J.T. It's only the boys runnin' the gauntlet."

"The gauntlet. I heard you mention that to Billy. Just what is this gauntlet you're talkin' about?"

"Come on. I'll show you."

Leading Toby, John Thomas followed Covington the length of the building and around to the open prairie in back. As the next Ranger prepared for his turn, Abe Covington explained how the gauntlet worked.

It had been the idea of the famed Ranger Leander McNelly. The course was one hundred yards long. There were a total of ten fence posts, with five on the right and five on the left, spaced a distance of ten yards apart. A target was placed on top of each post. Today it was watermelons. The rider would mount his horse twenty-five yards from the start of the course, draw two pistols, then spurring his horse into a full gallop, ride down the center of the gauntlet firing left and right in an attempt to hit as many targets as possible in the least amount of time. The gauntlet tested not only a man's marksmanship, but his horsemanship as well. It was an exercise that had proven its worth, the skills it sharpened taking a deadly toll countless times in running gun battles with Comanches, Apaches, and Mexican bandits.

Ranger Tom Overhalt was the next man up. As he mounted his horse at the far end of the course, J.T. pulled a slim cigar from his coat and lit up while he waited for the action to begin.

The Ranger checked his pistols, then with a yell, put spurs to the big roan he was riding. The horse leaped forward and was at a full gallop by the time horse and rider approached the first post, which came up on the right. Overhalt's first shot from the right-hand gun shattered the first melon. A cheer rose from his comrades, but there was no time for taking bows. At a full gallop the posts would be coming up fast, only seconds apart.

With the other gun in his left hand, the Ranger fired as he flew past the second post, but he missed this time. Then back to the right, a hit. Back and forth it went until Overhalt raced past the final post on the left. Altogether he had hit six out of ten. All in all, that wasn't that bad given the rigors of the test.

A small curl of smoke rose from the corner of J.T.'s lip as Covington said, "Well, that's the gauntlet. What'd you think?"

Removing the cigar from his mouth, J.T. nodded. "I'm impressed. You say McNelly came up with this idea? How's he doin' these days?"

"Not good, John T. That damn tuberculosis has wore

him down to nothin'. Don't figure he's got much longer."

"Damn shame. Figured a hard charger like Captain McNelly would go out in a blaze of glory with his boots on and his pistols hot. Don't seem right somehow."

Abe Covington kicked at the dirt along the fence, his tone expressing a deep-felt sadness as he answered. "Yeah, I know. He was always the one out front when the action started. Said a leader couldn't lead from the rear. He needed to be out front to set the example. Show his boys he wouldn't send 'em anywhere he wouldn't go himself. Sure gonna miss him when he's gone."

"Not only you boys, but the state of Texas as well," said J.T.

Billy Tyler was the next rider up.

"The kid any good at this?" asked J.T.

Covington showed a shy grin. "Watch, then you tell me."

A cheer went up from the Rangers as the boy started his run. Billy's horse was at full stride as he entered the gauntlet. The kid seemed to be moving at twice the speed of the previous rider, but young Billy appeared perfectly comfortable and confident as he snapped off his shots right, then left. By the time he had completed the run, eight of the ten melons lay scattered at the base of the posts.

Covington was still grinning. "Well, what d'you think?"

J.T. pushed his hat back with the tip of his finger. "I'd say the boy's a natural with those pistols. Good instincts and one hell of a horseman."

Billy Tyler walked up to the two men just as J.T. had finished his statement. The kid was beaming from ear to ear. "What d'ya think of that, J.T.? Not bad, huh?"

Remembering Abe's comment about the young lad's cockiness, J.T. replied, "Not bad, kid. But those two you missed would have more than likely drilled you right out of the saddle. So I guess it don't really matter now, does it?"

Billy's smile vanished, replaced now by a look of hurt pride.

"Oh, an I reckon ya could do better? Ain't nobody busted all ten at a full run 'ceptin' Cap'in McNelly, an' he only done it twice. Eight outta ten's just as good, I tell ya. Ain't that right, Abe?"

Covington knew what J.T. was up to and went right along with him. "Well, Billy. Mr. Law here is right 'bout one thing. Eight outta ten still leaves two fellas to leave you on the ground stone-cold dead."

Billy kicked the dirt with his boot. "Well, gaddammit! I got ten dollars here says there ain't nobody can hit ten outta ten at a full run." Looking straight at J.T., he continued. "An' I mean nobody!"

The Rangers had overheard the conversation, and began to gather around. There was no doubt that Billy had clearly challenged the bounty man and was putting up hard money to back up his words.

J.T. only grinned and shook his head.

"Now come on, Billy," said Overhalt. "You know you can't afford to lose no ten dollars. Hell, we was lucky to get paid at all this month. Don't go throwin' it away on some bet."

But Billy Tyler wasn't about to let this thing go. "So what d'ya say, J.T. Yer a gamblin' man, right? Folks say ya don't do nothin' for free. Well, here's ten dollars hard money. Ya game?"

There was a long moment of silence. All eyes were on the bounty hunter. J.T. looked over at Covington. "What'd you think, Abe?"

"Hey, it's your call, J.T., but the kid's right. McNelly's

the only person to ever go ten for ten since we started this thing, an' that's been awhile back."

J.T. thought on it for a few seconds, then tossing his half-finished cigar on the ground, removed his coat and handed it over to Covington. As J.T. swung up into the saddle, Toby snorted and pawed at the ground as if he too somehow sensed the challenge. Wheeling the big buckskin about, J.T. headed for the starting line.

"Looks like you got yourself a bet, Mr. Tyler," said Covington.

"Hot damn! This oughta be good. Come on!" shouted one of the Rangers.

While the targets were being set, J.T. checked his pistols, then gently rubbed his horse's neck while they waited. Billy Tyler finally signaled that all was ready. Still stroking Toby's neck, J.T. rapped the reins around the saddlehorn and leaned forward.

"Okay, fella, let's go all out. No slacking on the run, okay?"

Toby didn't disappoint his rider. One touch of the spurs and he leaped forward and broke straight into a dead run for the center of the gauntlet.

"Jesus, look at that horse move!" said one of the Rangers.

"Faster than anything we got in the barn, that's for damn sure," said another.

J.T. snapped off his first shot to the right. A hit dead center. The second shot to the left was also right on. Numbers three and four, five and six were equally impressive shots. With only four targets left, J.T. figured he'd give the Rangers a little special demonstration for their enjoyment. As numbers seven and eight came up, J.T. leaned all the way forward and firing from under the horse's neck, demolished both the right and left targets. For nine and ten, he sat upright for a moment, swung his right leg over the horse, and fired across the saddle, sending number nine into a hundred pieces. Then, in a quick and smooth movement, he swung over to the other side and hit number ten dead center as well.

Tyler and the other Rangers all stood in stunned silence. Even Abe Covington was at a loss for words. He knew J.T. was good, but he'd had no idea he was that good.

"That fella's ex-cavalry. Ain't no doubt about it," said Overhalt.

Another Ranger rubbed at his chin as he watched J.T. wheel the buckskin around and start back. "Ain't just any cavalry either, boys. Last time I saw anybody could ride and shoot like that was during the war. Guerrilla fighters outta Kansas and Missouri."

Billy Tyler's eyes lit up. "Ya mean Will Quantrill and Bloody Bill Anderson? And them fellas?"

"That's right, boy. Shootin' from the saddle, them boys was deadlier than a two-headed rattlesnake. Some of 'em carried six or eight guns with 'em, an' damn accurate with 'em too. An' they weren't near as good a pistol as we got now."

Abe Covington stood listening to the talk without saying anything. But he was thinking about it. He'd never heard John Thomas Law talk about the war or his part in it. But Law had gone to Kansas when he'd lost his ranch after the war, and had come back to Texas with a nice sum of money. That was another thing he never talked about. How he'd made his money while he was up there.

"Yes, sir. I'd bet my horse and rig that fellow rode with one of them outfits in the war," said the chin-rubber.

"Ya want I should ask him?" said Billy.

The question brought a clamor of negative responses from the group.

"Hell, no, boy! Ya' don't go proddin' into a man's past' lessen he brings it up his own self." Chin-Rubber's hand dropped quickly from his chin to Billy's arm. "Now don't you go sayin' nothin', Billy Tyler. I was just thinkin' out loud, that's all. I could be all wrong. So don't you be sayin' nothin' 'bout guerrillas or Quantrill or Bloody Bill, you hear?"

"That's right," said another. "The men that rode with those boys were like a keg of powder on a short fuse. Don't take much to set 'em off neither. Best to just leave it be."

As J.T. was approaching, Covington spoke up.

"Charlie's right, boys. War's been over a long time. No need in bringin' up the past. But I think we do owe Mr. Law a little show of appreciation for some fancy shootin'. What'd you say?"

As J.T. and Toby rode up, the Rangers gave them a short but polite round of applause. J.T. smiled, took his hat off, and gave a bow from the saddle. But as he replaced his hat and looked down at the group, he sensed that something was different. It took him a moment to figure it out. It was in their faces. They were all staring up at him, but there was something different about the way they looked at him. As if he wasn't even the same person that had taken Billy Tyler's bet on minutes earlier. Even Abe Covington.

John Thomas had learned you could tell a lot about a man by his eyes. Abe's eyes right now seemed full of questions. The others were the same. He even noted some glares of hostility from a few. He had no idea what had happened in the short span of ten minutes to warrant this new attitude, but whatever it was, no one seemed willing to talk about it right now.

Billy Tyler stepped forward. There was no problem with guessing the look in *his* eyes. If Sam Houston himself had been sitting there, the kid couldn't have been more in awe of a person as he now was of John Thomas

Law. Billy reached out his hand holding the ten dollars.

"Mr. Law, sir. I want ya to know I ain't never seen ridin' or shootin' like that in my life an' it's a damn pleasure to know ya."

J.T. grinned. "You keep your money, Billy. I needed the exercise."

Billy Tyler wasn't going to be refused. "No, sir. Ya won her fair and square. Hell, I'd'a paid ten dollars to watch ya do that anyway. So ya take her now. I mean it. A bet's a bet."

Leaning forward in the saddle, J.T. reluctantly accepted the money.

As Billy and the other Rangers went back to their practice, Abe said, "Well, I'd say you just grew about ten feet taller in that kid's eyes."

"Aw, he'll grow out of it. Here, take this ten dollars and use it to buy the boys some beer tonight. Now, if you don't have anything else, I'd like to get that bath, something to eat, and some sleep."

Abe paused a moment and stared up at J.T. There was that look again.

"You got something you want to ask me, Abe?"

The Ranger gently rubbed Toby's neck. "Naw, it's nothin' at all, J.T. Thanks for the donation. Come by the office when you're ready to head out. I'll have the warrants for the Baxters. See you later."

AFTER STABLING HIS horse, J.T. headed for the Manor House, one of the finer hotels in Austin. It boasted a first-rate staff, hot baths, and the softest flat-ironed sheets in Texas. The price was steep—thirty dollars a night. But it was a price that guaranteed the caliber of its clientele.

Walking into the lobby, John Thomas paused to admire the place. A huge round settee with a host of bright green trees, plants, and palms in the center occupied a large portion of the lobby. Scattered at different locations along the walls were large overstuffed chairs and sofas of various colors, covered with the finest materials. Hanging from a large center beam was a triple-level glass chandelier with three to four hundred teardrop-shaped pieces of crystal hanging from each circle, from the smallest circle at the top to the largest at the bottom, which appeared to be at least eight feet wide. It was a pretty damn impressive place to say the least.

Walking toward the front desk J.T. watched as the short, balding desk clerk forced a smile, adjusted his tie, and turned the guest register around for the approaching J.T. to sign.

Dropping his saddlebags on the counter, J.T. picked up the pen that was attached to the book by a long thin gold chain and said, "Afternoon. You got anything open on the top floor?"

The clerk cleared his throat in an obvious gesture to get J.T.'s attention. Looking up from the book, J.T. saw the prim and proper clerk eyeing, as if in silent pain, the dust-covered saddlebags that had suddenly invaded his personal realm of spit and polish. Displaying a half smile, J.T. lifted the weather-worn and dust-covered bags from the counter and placed them beside him on the floor.

"Sorry, friend. Been a while since I been under a roof."

"That's quite all right, sir," came the reply from the clerk, who had suddenly produced a cloth from out of nowhere and already wiped away any sign of J.T.'s thoughtless indiscretion.

Placing the pen back in the book, J.T. said, "I'd like to get a bath as soon as possible, and I'll need someone to come by the room later. I've got some clothes that'll need lots of soap and water."

"Certainly, sir. Now, let's see. You said something on the top floor. Front or rear, sir?"

"Front, if you have it."

As the clerk turned to the rows of slotted boxes that held the room keys, J.T. flipped a page back in the register, more from habit than curiosity. His eyes quickly scanned the page, then suddenly stopped as he saw a name that he recognized. Mr. C. T. Taylor of Springfield, Missouri. When the clerk returned with his key, J.T. asked, "How long has Mr. Taylor of Springfield been here?"

Swinging the book back his way, the clerk studied it a moment, then answered, "Came in yesterday morning with two other gentlemen. Friends of yours, sir?"

"I'm not sure. The name's familiar."

"I'm afraid they've stepped out. Saw them leave around noon. You could leave a message if you like. I'll see that Mr. Taylor gets it as soon as he returns."

"No. That's all right. Might not be the same fellow I'm thinkin' of anyway. But thanks. How long for the bath?"

"About an hour, Mr. . . . uh . . ." The clerk quickly glanced at the book. "Uh, Mr. Law."

The man's face seem to lose some of its color as he read the name again. Looking up, he asked, "That wouldn't happen to be John Thomas Law by chance, would it, sir?"

"That's the name. Is there a problem?"

There was a sudden nervousness in the man's voice. "No . . . no, sir. I'll send the boy up for your clothes when the bath is ready, Mr. Law. Yes, sir. Anything you might need, please let me know, sir."

J.T. thanked the man and with his saddlebags trailing dust behind him, made his way up the stairs. The clerk never took his eyes off him until he was out of sight.

The room was every bit as elaborate as the lobby. Polished mahogany nightstands on each side of the bed. A fully supplied writing desk. Lace curtains on the windows, tied back with satin sashes. A complimentary bottle of whiskey with crystal glasses and a box of cigars sat on a table next to a chest of drawers. There was a large overstuffed chair in the corner, a sofa against one wall, and a large four-poster bed with a canopy against another wall. It was almost too nice. Suddenly conscious of the trail dust not only on himself, but on the saddlebags as well, J.T. looked for a place to put them down that wouldn't leave a mess, but everything was so damn clean. Then it hit him.

"Hell fire. What's wrong with me? I'm paying thirty dollars a day for this place!"

That realization quickly replaced the awe and wonder of only a moment ago. With a heave, he tossed the bags onto the chair. Taking off his coat, he tossed it on the sofa. Walking over to the bottle of whiskey, he poured himself a tall glass, then went over and sat on the bed. It was the first time he had really relaxed since he had arrived in Austin. Like everything else about the Manor House, the whiskey was of the finest quality, and went down smooth, not like that snakebite stuff Abe Covington had given him. Easing himself back on the bed, he continued to sip at the whiskey. He couldn't help but think what a difference the passing years had made in his life. He had gone from a flat-broke Johnny Reb without a home, to a respected and feared gunfighter who was now drinking fine whiskey in a thirty-dollar-a-day room in one of the best hotels in Texas while someone was busy preparing a hot bath for him. It just didn't get any better than this.

A knock at the door brought J.T. straight off the bed. The second glass of that smooth Tennessee whiskey had relaxed him to a point where he had simply lain back onto the soft confines of that big four-poster bed and drifted off to sleep.

There was a second knock, louder this time. As he started to rise, he looked down to find the short-barreled Colt in his right hand. He didn't even remember drawing the pistol. It had simply been instinct.

Moving to the door, he cocked the Colt and placed his right hand behind his back. A man in his profession could just as easily get shot dead in a fancy hotel as he could in a saloon. Stepping to the side of the door, J.T. asked, "Who is it?"

"The porter, sir. Your bath is ready. The front desk said you had some clothes you wanted sent out for washing and cleaning. I'll pick those up now if that is all right with you, sir."

With the gun still behind his back, J.T. opened the door to find a young man of sixteen or seventeen, dressed in black pants, white shirt, and a bright red vest, standing there holding some towels. The boy's smile suddenly faded when his eyes noticed the empty shoulder holster and J.T. with his hand behind his back. Taking a step back from the doorway, the boy stammered, "I . . . I can come back later, sir. If . . . if you like. I'm sorry I disturbed you, sir."

J.T. tried to ease the boy's mind with a friendly grin.

"No, that's fine, boy. I was just cleaning my gun. Sorry if I gave you a bit of a start there. Come on in, I'll just be a minute."

Pushing the Colt back into place, J.T. pulled all the clothes from his saddlebags, setting aside his last clean shirt, pants, and vest. He stripped down, tossed the clothes he had been wearing onto the pile with the others, and said, "Well, reckon that's about it."

The boy moved to the bed, placed the towels on the nightstand, then shoved all the dirty clothes into a pillowcase. Spying the black frock coat on the sofa, he asked, "The coat as well, sir?"

"Sure thing. Damn near forgot about that."

The lad quickly went through the pockets to assure that there was nothing in them, then placed it in with the rest.

"Okay, sir. If there's nothing else. You'll find a robe in the closet and your bath ready at the end of the hall. I'll have these things back to you by noon tomorrow. I hope that will be sufficient."

John Thomas was impressed. The boy's manner was every bit as smooth as the whiskey. Taking three silver dollars from the money on the bed, J.T. placed them in the boy's hand.

"That'll be just fine, son."

The smile was back as the boy replied, "Thank you, sir."

J.T. closed the door behind him as he left.

Opening the closet J.T. found the robe. He wasn't sure what it was made of, but it was sure enough soft and had the hotel's name monogrammed on the pocket. For a man who was accustomed to traipsing around in his long underwear or in the altogether, this robe business was a whole new experience, and one he wasn't all that comfortable with. If only Big Bertha and the girls at her whorehouse in Denver could see him now. They'd bust a gut laughing without a doubt. It was all he could do to keep from laughing himself when he saw himself in the mirror.

Taking the towels and a Colt with him, J.T. walked to the end of the hall. Inside, the door had a heavy bolt to assure privacy. Steam rose from the bathwater. There was an assortment of bottled bath oils on a tray next to the tub. Suddenly thirty dollars a day didn't seem like enough money for this kind of service.

Bolting the door, he placed the Colt on the tray next to

the bottles, making sure it was in easy reach once he was in the tub. Again, another natural survival instinct. No matter where he went or what he was doing, even taking time to enjoy a few of the finer things, J.T. Law knew he could never afford the luxury of relaxation without a gun being within easy reach. It was the price a man paid for his reputation and his chosen profession.

THREE

NATE BAXTER THREW a stack of bills on the bar and yelled out, "Drinks are on me, boys! Bartender—when that runs out ya let me know. I got plenty where that come from. Drink up, boys! Nate Baxter's back in town."

A wild cheer rose from the crowd as they stampeded to the bar. Nobody in the small town of Steeles Grove turned down a free drink. As word spread up and down the street, the saloon filled to elbow-room-only in record time.

Reaching over the bar, Nate pulled a bottle of whiskey and four glasses from the shelf. Pushing his way through the crowd, he made his way to a corner table in the back of the room. Setting the glasses on the table, he poured all four full to the brim, then sat down. Raising his glass, he looked into the faces of the three men sitting around him.

"To the Baxter brothers."

"Here, here!" said Charlie.

"Damn straight," cried Tom.

"Hell, yes!" came the reply from Coe, the youngest of the group.

The brothers downed their drinks and placed the glasses on the table, where they were quickly refilled by Tom Baxter.

Nate was the oldest and by far the meanest of the bunch. Not only did he have a quick temper, but he was also the best of the group with a six-gun or rifle. A veteran of the Southern cause, he had never forgiven Lee for surrendering to Grant at Appomattox Courthouse. Nate had returned to his home in Texas a bitter and resentful man. It was a nagging feeling that had brewed within him all these years, until finally something had snapped and all that bitterness and hatred was now being unleashed on the people of Texas.

Charlie was the next oldest. He too had ridden for the South, but unlike Nate, who had fought at places like Gettysburg, Shiloh, and Yellow Tavern, Charlie had never left the state of Texas. But he'd seen his share of Yankees during the war. The battles weren't as well known, but they were just as deadly. Dragoon Wells, Boones Pass, and Palmitto Ranch, the site of the last major land battle of the war. It was at the Battle of Comanche Pass that Charlie had been badly wounded. A bullet had shattered his jaw and taken off half of his left ear. The wound had put Charlie out of the war. And it was only after months of constant care by his family that Charlie fully recovered. It wasn't until Nate came home and began dogging him about his face and his ear that Charlie's resentment began to grow. Before long he was as bitter and filled with anger as Nate, and was looking for any excuse to vent that anger on someone. Then Nate had walked in one day and declared, "They owe us, by God! What d'ya say?"

Charlie had strapped on his gun and gone right along

with his older brother. Banks, stages, or trains, hell, it didn't matter anymore. Nate had him convinced that everyone was laughing at him and his damn funny-looking ear anyway.

Tom was too young to have fought in the war, but he had been in awe of his two older brothers and their stories of battles and adventure. He would listen for hours to their embellished tales and curse himself for not having been old enough to ride with them on those great adventures. It was only natural that when Nate and Charlie decided to go on their rampage, Tom was ready and willing to go along. True, it wasn't the War Between the States with all the chivalry and honor, but after all the hell they had raised in the last month, Tom had little doubt that a war of a different kind was headed their way and this time he'd be riding with his brothers.

Sitting next to Tom was Coe Baxter, the youngest of of the crew. Barely seventeen, he'd seen more dead people in the last month than he'd seen in his entire young life. The shame of what Nate and Charlie had done to that poor woman on the stage still bothered him. Gunplay against other men he could understand, but the terror and violation of a woman couldn't be justified no matter how he tried to look at it. Yet he knew what really bothered him was the fact that for all his moral ideals, he hadn't done anything to stop it. He'd walked away, not wanting to see or hear the laughing of his brothers nor the screaming and crying of the woman at their mercy. Even now, as they drank their whiskey, paid for by the blood of that woman and all the others who had been killed in the last few weeks, Coe Baxter tried to figure out how he'd gotten himself into this and why he was even here. He hadn't lost a war, been made fun of, or been mistreated by anyone in Texas. So what was he doing here?

As if by some strange premonition, the boy's answer

came walking toward him in the form of a bearded old man with dark-set eyes and a weathered face that had seen more than its share of hard times. This was Morgan Baxter, father of this outlaw brood. There wasn't one of the boys at the table who hadn't felt the sting of the thick leather barber's strap that hung by the front door of the Baxter ranch. Morgan Baxter was the real reason Coe had gone along with his brothers. The young boy would rather face the devil himself than the wrath of this old man.

Jerking an empty chair back from the table, the old man sat himself down. He pulled the bottle out of Tom's hand and taking Coe's glass, poured himself a healthy shot of whiskey and tossed it back. All conversation had stopped.

"Damn fool thing ya done, Nate. Wastin' good money like this. Buyin' a whole town drinks. What the hell was ya thinkin', boy?" asked the old man as he slammed the empty glass down on the table and stared across at his eldest son.

Nate avoided the old man's eyes and looked around the table at his brothers, but it was clear they weren't going to say a thing.

"Don't be lookin' to yer brothers, boy. I didn't ask them nothin'. I asked you. Ya gone dumb 'tween them ears or are ya just stupid drunk?"

Every nerve and muscle in Nate's body tensed. He'd like nothing better than to pull his Colt right now and blow this old man's head off. But all those years of backhanding and strap beatings had not been wasted on Nate, or the others for that matter. The old man had put the fear of God in each and every one of them. It wasn't the voice of a hardened killer that answered now.

"I figured if we kept the town folks on our side they might help us out sometime, like if the law come snoopin' around."

"Yeah, Pa," said Charlie. "Kinda like the folks up in Missouri do for Frank and Jesse James."

The old man burst out laughing, then staring Charlie down, growled, "Hell, you boys must be drunk or touched thinkin' ya can put yerself in the same company as Jesse and Frank James. Hell, you boys couldn't even clean the cowshit off'n their boots. They're real outlaws. They got a style and class all their own. That's what makes them boys heroes to folks—not free cheap whiskey and a lot of talk."

Nate came right back. "You just wait, Pa. We're just gettin' started. If we can keep the law off us, people'll be talkin' about us the same way one of these days. You just wait an' see."

"Damn right they will," said Charlie. "Just give us some time. That's all."

The old man downed another drink and slowly nodded his head. "Well, yer gonna have plenty of time without the law botherin' ya. Bunch of Comanches jumped the reservation up in the Nations. They're headed south. That'll keep the Rangers and the Army busy for a good spell. They ain't gonna be havin' no time to deal with you boys. Not for now anyway."

Nate leaned back in his chair and grinned. "The Lord sure does work in mysterious ways. That just about gives us a free hand to do any damn thing we have an urge to do, don't it?"

"Lord ain't got shit to do with it, Nate," barked the old man. "Just some bucks got an itch to be as famous as Sittin' Bull an' Crazy Horse are right now. They get done tanglin' with them Rangers, they'll be wishin' they was back on that damn reservation."

"Yeah, but till then we got a pretty free hand to do what we want."

"So what's yer next move, 'sides gettin' the whole

damn town drunk? Or have ya figured that far ahead yet?"

Nate nodded. "Got a bank up in Coal County that should be easy pickin's for four men. This is Tuesday. Figure to start up that way tomorrow afternoon. The farmers and ranchers will be puttin' their money in that bank Friday afternoon. We oughta be gettin' there just 'bout closin' time. Got a head banker, two tellers, and an old retired lawman they use for a guard. Don't really see no problem with that. Figure five minutes to be in and out of the bank. Place oughta be bustin' with money."

The old man poured drinks all around, then slapped his oldest son on the back. "Now ya see? That's how ya answer a man's question, boys. Y'all pay attention to Nate here an y'all learn somethin'."

Raising his glass, Morgan Baxter purposed a toast. "Here's to my boys. I'm damn proud of all of ya."

Five glasses clicked together over the center of the table amid a rousing cheer from all but one. Coe had waited all his life to hear those words, "I'm proud of you," from his father. But now, as he heard them, all he could see was a terrified woman screaming.

FOUR

FOLLOWING HIS BATH, J.T. had returned to his room and stretched out on the big four-poster bed before going to supper. But the combination of a warm bath and a soft bed had caused him to sleep the rest of the day and through the night. Instead of going to supper, he found himself having a late breakfast of steak, fried eggs, taters, and sourdough biscuits backed up with plenty of strong black coffee. The fourteen or so hours of undisturbed sleep and a fine meal had J.T. feeling like a new man. As the waitress cleared away the dishes and refilled his coffee cup, he sat back in his chair and lit up a slim cigar. For the moment he was fully content and all seemed right with the world. But of course that wasn't going to last for long.

Puffing away on his cigar, J.T. saw a familiar face appear in the doorway of the hotel restaurant. The man was well dressed in a suit, vest, and tie that fit his big frame well. Scanning the room, the man saw J.T. sitting at a corner table and headed that way. A big smile came over his face as he approached the table and extended his hand.

"John Thomas. How the hell are you, old friend?"

J.T. reached out and clasped the big hand in a firm grip. "Nice to see you again, Mr. Taylor. Been a long time. Have a seat. You like some coffee or something to eat?"

"Just coffee will do."

J.T. started to wave the waitress over, but there was no need. She was already coming their way with a cup and a pot of the steaming brew. As she filled both cups, both men sat silently staring at each other. Once she had left, J.T. was the first to speak.

"Saw the name on the register when I came in yesterday afternoon. Thought maybe that was you. Who's with you?"

Mr. Taylor took a sip of his coffee as he looked around the room checking out the other patrons before answering. "Jim and Bob. They got a little rowdy last night. Both got hangovers the size of Texas this morning. They're sleepin' in late."

Shifting his steel-blue eyes to J.T., he asked, "An' how about you, J.T.? What's it been, six—seven years now? What you been doin' with yourself?"

"Closer to eight," came the reply.

"God almighty. Been that long. Time sure seems to get away from me these days. Must be gettin' old. We heard you'd become a bounty hunter. An' a damn good one too. That right?"

J.T. gave a slight grin as he nodded. "That's right. But how good I am is a matter of opinion. Don't worry. I limit my work to Texas and the Nations up in Indian territory. Haven't been up Kansas or Missouri way in a lot of years."

Now it was Taylor who was grinning. "That's good, J.T. There's still a few folks up that way still lookin' for a fella that comes right close to fittin' your description."

"Do tell."

"Sure enough. Seems they want to talk to this fellow up in Kansas. Something about an Army payroll him and five other boys stole. An' in Missouri, I think they mentioned something about a bank owned by a bunch of Northern businessmen bein' robbed. Course that's been a while back, but you know how some of them Yankees are. They just can't seem to forgive or forget."

J.T. nodded. "Yeah, I sure know how that is. But I'd think those folks wouldn't have time to worry about eight or nine years ago. Figure they'd have their hands full trying to handle those boys that have been raisin' hell up that way for the last ten years."

J.T. paused a second as if trying to remember a name, then continued. "Let's see now. What were those names again. Oh, yeah. That damn bunch of hooligans, the James and Younger gang. I believe that's what they call 'em."

Taylor laughed. "Hell, they call 'em a lot worse than that. They just can't print words like that in a newspaper."

"I hear tell this Jesse James runs a pretty tight outfit."

Some of the humor left Taylor's face. "Yeah. But I hear he's been pushin' damn hard on some of them boys. There's talk of a split comin' if he don't let up on some of 'em soon."

J.T. stared down at his coffee cup. "Sorry to hear that. Understand they been together a long time."

"Yeah, played together since they were kids. But time changes a lot of things, J.T. Maybe it's time they went their separate ways before there's any hard feelings."

J.T. wasn't sure what to say to that, so he simply didn't say anything.

Abe Covington came through the door and spying J.T.,

walked up to his table. He held some folded papers in his hand.

"Mornin', J.T. Sorry to interrupt your breakfast."

"That's no problem, Abe, already finished. You like to join us for some coffee?"

As was his normal custom, Abe gave the man in the suit a quick appraisal, taking in his features, which seemed somehow familiar to him. Without taking his eyes off Taylor, he replied, "No, thanks, J.T. We're headin' out after Iron Hand this morning. I just wanted to make sure you got your warrants for the Baxters before I left."

J.T. took the papers and shoved them into his coat pocket. "Abe, this here is C.T. Taylor. He's a cattle buyer out of Springfield, Missouri. C.T., this is Abe Covington, head of the Texas Rangers here."

The two men shook hands.

"Have we ever met before, Mr. Taylor?" ask Covington.

"No, sir. Not that I recollect. This here's the first time I been down this way. Normally do business in Dallas or Fort Worth. Matter of fact, I'm leaving this morning myself. Headin' back to Springfield."

Abe nodded, but it was clear the Ranger was still trying to place where he'd see Taylor before. Slapping J.T. on the back, Abe said, "Gotta' get movin', John T. You remember what I said about that bunch and good luck to you."

"You too, Abe. Make sure you hang onto your hair."

After Abe had left, Taylor said, "Seems like a nice enough fellow for a lawman."

"He is that. An' dedicated to his job too. He sure gave you a pretty good going over. You can bet he'll file your description away for later reference."

"Good thing we're leavin' this mornin' then. Reckon I

better head up to the room and get them boys movin'. We gotta be back in Missouri in two days."

"Got an appointment, do you?"

Taylor finished the last of his coffee. "Yeah, Clell Miller's got some folks up Minnesota way that say there's plenty of business opportunities in a town called Northfield. Some of my friends wanta ride up that way and check it out."

J.T. got a sudden chill down his back. He couldn't explain it, but there was something about the name Northfield that had set it off. Hell, he'd never heard of the place nor had he ever been to Minnesota, so he couldn't explain why it bothered him.

"Sounds like it's a long way from Missouri. Maybe too far."

J.T. saw a worried look come over Taylor's face. "Yeah, I know. If we weren't already committed, I swear I'd pass on this business trip. We got plenty of business close to home. But what are you gonna do? You tell a man you'll do something—you do it."

Getting up from the table, the two men walked out into the lobby. Shaking hands, Taylor said, "John T., it's been a pleasure to see you again. Brought back a lot of memories of the good times. Abe Covington was right. You watch your ass with them Baxters. Heard some folks talkin' about 'em last night. Sound like a downright dangerous bunch. Hell, we didn't have to leave today, we'd go with you."

Pumping his friend's hand with a firm grip, J.T. smiled. "Don't mind sayin' you'd be welcome company. But I understand. A man gives his word, he has to stand by it. Good luck to you. An' tell Jesse and Frank I said howdy from Texas when you see them, okay?"

"I sure will, John. You take care of yourself."

As the two parted company, J.T. watched the man

known as C.T. Taylor walk up the stairs to wake his brothers, Jim and Bob. Pausing at the top of the landing, the big man turned and waved one last time. As J.T. waved back, he somehow knew that this would be the last time he would ever see his old friend and wartime comrade Cole Younger.

FIVE

★

J.T. LEFT THE Manor House that afternoon. He was fully rested, had fresh-smelling, clean clothes, and carried warrants worth four thousand dollars in his coat pocket. It was now time to go to work. Abe and all but a skeleton crew of Rangers had already headed north in search of the Comanches. Cole Younger and his brothers were on their way back to Missouri, and J.T. Law was heading for east Texas and the town of Nacogdoches. It was the last place the Baxter brothers had been seen and as good a place as any to start his search.

As he rode east, the big news in every town he passed through was the Comanche breakout. Suddenly people were seeing Indians everywhere. Exaggerated tales of massacres and scalping were running rampant, adding to the hysteria. Normally quiet little towns had become armed forts overnight. With each town he rode through the rumored number of Comanches on the loose increased. It had gone from the original seventy-five to a hundred to well over a thousand by the time he had reached Nacogdoches. There were even rumors that Crazy Horse himself was leading a party of over one thousand Sioux down from Montana to join forces with the Comanches. As J.T. had told Abe Covington earlier, it had been a long time since there had been any Indian trouble in Texas, and the mass hysteria going on now was proof of that.

The town of Nacogdoches was no different. Men with rifles strolled the rooftops, keeping a watchful eye on the vast empty plains that surrounded the town. Barricades had been erected along some of the storefronts, and city officials had placed a huge bell in the middle of Main Street to sound the warning of an impending attack.

Hardly anyone noticed J.T. as he hitched his horse in front of the sheriff's office and went inside. A heavyset man with graying salt-and-pepper hair and wearing a badge sat at a desk. A variety of shotguns, rifles, and pistols covered the desktop. The lawman was busy loading the weapons from a stack of boxes that were piled high next to his chair. He glanced up as J.T. entered, then went on about the business of shoving shells into a Winchester as he asked, "Somethin' I can do for you, mister?"

"I'm looking for the sheriff."

"That'd be me. Name's Willard Bowlin."

J.T. pulled up a chair and sat down in front of the desk. "I understand two Texas Rangers were killed here a few weeks ago. That right?"

The lawman paused a moment and looked over at his visitor. He was looking for a badge. "You a Texas Ranger?"

"Nope. But one of those Rangers killed was a friend of mine. I'd like to know what you've done about it."

The man suddenly averted his eyes from J.T. and went

back to loading the rifle. "I'm still investigatin' that killing. Can't seem to find no witnesses."

John T. felt a knot form in the pit of his stomach. "If you don't mind me saying so, you must not be much at investigating, Sheriff."

The man's head snapped up. J.T. had his full attention now.

"An' just what the hell's that suppose to mean?"

J.T. leaned forward in the chair, his face hard and his eyes fixed squarely on the lawman.

"Means you're either on the Baxters' payroll or they got you buffaloed. Which one is it, Sheriff?"

Bowlin's face went beet red. He levered a shell into the chamber of the Winchester and slowly began moving the barrel of the rifle around toward J.T. In the blink of an eye, the Colt from the shoulder rig was in the bounty man's hand, cocked and pointed straight at Bowlin's head.

"You move that Winchester one more inch an' they'll be cleanin' your brains off the walls. Now put that rifle on the desk an' be damn careful how you go about it."

Bowlin slowly turned the rifle to the side and carefully placed it in the center of the desk. "Just who the hell are you, mister?"

Pulling the warrants from his coat pocket, J.T. tossed them on the pile of weapons. "Name's John Thomas Law and I've got warrants on all four of the Baxter brothers. So where are they?"

Bowlin leaned back in his chair. With a look of pure disgust on his face he muttered, "Goddamn bounty hunter. Didn't take you long to come crawlin' out from under your rock, did it, bounty man?"

J.T. had to give Bowlin credit. That wasn't the kind of remark many men would make looking down the barrel of a cocked .45.

"About as long as it took you and that badge to slip

under the same rock with the Baxters. Now that we got the insults out of the way, where are they?"

"How the hell should I know! They come ridin' in here couple weeks ago big as brass an' throwin' money around like it was nothin'. Next I know I got two Rangers an' a whore from Mattie's dead down by the stockyards."

"Hell, Bowlin. Everybody in this town knew who did it. Why didn't you arrest them when you had the chance?"

The sheriff shook his head from side to side as he grunted out a laugh. "Yeah. Well that's easy for you to say, J.T. Law. You got the balls of a bull moose and an eagle eye that can knock the pimple off a fly's ass with them Colts of yours. But you see, I ain't no damn hero. My eyes are bad an' I'm damn lucky if I can hit a barn door with six shots. You think what you want, bounty hunter, but at least I ain't layin' in that cemetery out there with your Ranger friends."

At least the man was honest. Lowering the hammer on the gun, J.T. slid it back into place in the shoulder holster. He didn't figure he'd need it anymore. He'd made his point.

"You got any idea where they might have gone when they left here?"

Bowlin shook his head. "Not sure, mind you. But if I had to guess, I'd say they headed for home."

"An' just where might that be?"

"Place called Steeles Grove down in Tyler County. Like I said, I ain't swearin' to it, but it's a damn good bet they'll show up there sooner or later to see their pa."

J.T. stood and walked to the door. As he opened it, he paused and looked back at Bowlin. "You might wanta load all those rifles. Heard a rumor up in Austin that those Comanche were talking about this town when they busted out."

J.T. gained a measure of satisfaction watching Bowlin's face turn an ashen gray at the very thought of an Indian attack on his town. Closing the door behind him, J.T. headed across the street to Mattie's Saloon. It was a busy place, filled to the walls. A piano player was trying in vain to play above the din of yelling, laughing cowboys, but had lost that battle long ago.

As the batwing doors swung behind him, J.T. saw several men look in his direction. One cowboy jumped up from a table and moved quickly to the bar. He said something to two other men. They looked his way, then hurried out the back.

It was apparent by the looks and whispering going on around the tables that a lot of people knew who he was and exactly why he was in Nacogdoches. One person who was particularly interested in the bounty hunter was a big-breasted woman in a tight-fitting red dress that was straining to keep her assets from popping out every time she moved. Getting a bottle and two glasses from the bartender, she cut J.T. off before he reached the bar.

"Hi there, bounty man. You got a minute for an old gal with a bottle of her private stock?"

J.T. figured there had to be two inches of powder and makeup on her face. But as rough around the edges as she appeared, she had the softest, caring eyes he had seen in a long time. Removing his hat and trying hard not to stare at her chest, he replied, "I appreciate the offer, but I'm here to see Miss Mattie."

"Well, then, you got plenty of time, sweetie. I'm Mattie. Come on, follow me."

The woman pushed and bumped her way through the crowd to a door near the end of the bar. Grabbing J.T. by the arm, she pulled him into the room behind her. It was Mattie's office. The strong scent of cheap perfume hung heavy in the room. Leading him to a sofa, she pushed him back onto it, then dropped down beside him. Opening the whiskey, she poured both glasses half full and handed one to John Thomas.

"So you were comin' to see me, were you, John T.?"

"Sheriff said it was one of your girls that got herself killed with those two Rangers a while back. I wanted to ask you some questions about the men that did it."

A look of pure hate appeared in the woman's eyes. "The goddamn Baxter brothers. They're all a bunch of low-life sonsabitches. I hope to hell those Comanche catch their sorry asses and roast their balls off over a slow-burnin' spit." She paused a second, "Well, all of 'em except maybe young Coe. That kid's got no business bein' with that bunch. He ain't mean enough."

J.T. found this interesting. It was the first halfway decent thing he'd heard said about any of the bunch. "Why do you say that, Mattie?"

"Night of the killin's, Coe came right here to this office. He had tears in his eyes when he told me how sorry he was about my poor, sweet Ruby. They'd been together a few times. He liked her, an' I think she liked him more'n she put on. You know what that kid done? Give me five hundred dollars to send to Ruby's folks. Didn't want me to tell nobody. That sound like a hardcase killer to you?"

"None I've had to deal with. I'll keep that in mind when I catch up to 'em."

"You goin' after that bunch by yourself? Hell, John T., that makes you a bigger fool than I thought. That'd be four against one, maybe five if their old man's with 'em."

J.T.'s expression never changed. Everyone had a right to their opinion. "This boy, Coe. He give you any idea where they might be headed when they left here?"

Mattie could tell that this was a stubborn man. Once he set his mind to do something, he'd see it through to the end no matter what the odds. He was handsome, strong, polite, but all business. Rare qualities when compared to the men she had to deal with on a daily basis. Before this night she had only known him by reputation, but years of experience in her line of work had shown her that most men with supposed reputations didn't measure up in the end. This J.T. Law was definitely not one of those. If anyone could stand up to the Baxters, it would be this man.

"You're serious, ain't you. You're really gonna take 'em all on by yourself."

"Yes, I am, Mattie. They've killed a lot of people. Somebody has to put an end to it. Figure it might as well be me. Now, did Coe say anything before he left?"

"They were going home. Some half-ass town called Steeles Grove, I believe. You find 'em, J.T., you kill that damn Tom Baxter for sure. He's the one that put Ruby up to that business with them Rangers. Bastard knew she'd get killed, but he didn't give a damn about that. She wouldn't have been there if it hadn't been for that smooth-talkin' bastard. You promise me that, okay?"

J.T. could see the pain in those soft eyes when she spoke of the girl called Ruby. Getting to his feet, J.T. replied, "I'll promise you this, Mattie. He'll get what's comin' to him, one way or the other."

Walking him to the door, she placed her hand on his arm as he was leaving.

"Good luck to you, J.T. Law. An' bless you."

SIX

STEELES GROVE WAS the typical small hamlet that had sprung up at a crossroads leading to bigger towns. They did a robust business in livestock and mercantile, selling to the constant flow of settlers and wagon trains heading in all directions across the vast reaches of Texas in search of their future. From a small two-room trading post had sprung a town, complete with church, school, shops, saloons, and even a courthouse. Folks said you could tell a place had become a regular full-fledged town when it could boast it had more than two lawyers. Steeles Grove had four.

It was mid-morning when J.T. reached the outskirts of the town, halting to make the traditional check of his hardware. The Colts were primed and ready and so was he. Heading Toby down the main street, he quickly realized from the stares he was receiving that the people of this town had known he was coming. He thought back to that night at Mattie's and the three cowboys who had left so quickly by the back door when he had entered. It was a good bet they had left Nacogdoches and headed straight for Steeles Grove to warn the Baxters. That was all just theory, of course, but one way or the other, somehow these people knew they could expect a visit from a bounty hunter.

Reining up in front of the sheriff's office, J.T. stepped down and flipped Toby's reins around the hitch rail. Up and down the street small groups of people were gathering and beginning to move toward the sheriff's office. They knew who this stranger was, all right, and they wanted to let him know it.

Not one to be intimidated, J.T. pulled out one of his favorite slim cigars. Taking his time to light it, he studied the faces of the crowd gathering around him. Most seemed to be just everyday folks, but there were a number of tough-looking men among them who were more than likely friends of the Baxter boys. Those were the ones he'd have to keep an eye on while he was in town. Taking a puff of the cigar, J.T. rubbed Toby's mane and whispered, "Don't think we're very welcome here, Toby. But then, that's never stopped us before, has it, fella?"

J.T. was about to step up on the boardwalk in front of the sheriff's office when the door opened and out stepped a burly bear of a man with a tin star on his chest. The man had to stand six feet six, and looked to weigh an easy three hundred pounds. He had an old-model Colt .44 strapped to his leg and held a double-barrel Greener scattergun in his hand, the barrels pointing down for the moment. To J.T., standing in the street and looking up, the lawman looked like a giant. A sizable crowd had now gathered around J.T., and they were all watching and waiting for their sheriff to speak. When he did, it was in a low, threatening tone that was anything but friendly.

"You that bounty hunter I been hearin' about for two damn days?"

J.T. took a step back to put a little distance between him and the giant. Taking a quick glance to his left and right, he looked back at the lawman.

"They seem to think so."

"Your name J.T. Law?" boomed the voice from above.

"It is. An' I'm here to serve warrants issued by the state of Texas for the arrest of Nate, Charlie, Tom, and Coe Baxter for robbery, rape, and murder."

The sheriff spat a stream of tobacco juice inches from J.T.'s left boot. "Do tell. An' just what the hell you expect me to do about all that?"

J.T. took another two steps back, calculating the angle he'd have to use to hit this big ox between the eyes with his first shot if the sheriff brought that shotgun up in his direction. It was a move that didn't go unnoticed by the sheriff or the people in the crowd. Those standing directly behind J.T. parted like the Red Sea, making sure they would be out of harm's way of any shotgun blast.

J.T. glanced down at the near miss by his boot. Then straight into the lawman's eyes.

"Texas law says I got to notify the local authorities when there are outstanding warrants for any of their citizens. I see it more as a professional courtesy than a requirement. But I can see any courtesy, professional or otherwise, would be wasted on an ignorant son of a bitch like you."

A sudden murmur rose from the crowd of onlookers. One said, "Damn, the man's got sand, I'll give him that."

J.T. could tell by the lawman's eyes that he was mad as hell, but not sure what to do about it. The bounty man's reputation for steel nerve and lightning speed with those .45's was well known. The sheriff also realized too late that he had lost the early advantage by allowing J.T. to take those three steps back. The question now was, could he swing the shotgun up before the gunfighter could draw and fire?

J.T. saw the man's finger tense, then slowly tighten on the triggers of the scattergun. The big ox was about to try his luck. At this distance, even if J.T. hit him square between the eyes, reflex action would pull those triggers and possibly take J.T.'s legs off at the knees. He saw the man's wrist begin to arch.

J.T. leaped forward, pushing the shotgun barrel aside with his right hand while drawing his Peacemaker with the other and bringing it up with all his might between the sheriff's legs. In the next instant both barrels of the shotgun exploded, the buckshot shattering a barrel of apples sitting in front of the general store, sending a shower of pulp and wood in all directions. At the same time came a loud, sorrowful moan and the sound of air leaving the sheriff's body.

The ox dropped to his knees, crying out in pain. J.T. then brought the barrel of the .45 around from the side as hard as he could. There was a sickening crack as the barrel struck the man full force in the side of the head. The blow rendered him unconscious. He fell forward, landing face-first in the street.

J.T. quickly moved up on the walkway, both Colts now in his hands, ready for whatever was going to happen next. But there was nothing. He found himself facing a shocked and totally stunned crowd.

"Some of you folks might wanta get this man out of the street and to a doctor. The rest of you go on about your business. The show's over."

A small army of men moved forward and with great effort, managed to pick the sheriff up and carry him down the street to the doctor's office. A large portion of the crowd followed along, while the rest went back to what they'd been doing before the bounty man had arrived. Holstering his pistols, J.T. picked up the shotgun and went straight into the sheriff's office. A few minutes later he came back out still carrying the scattergun and two boxes of double-aught buck. Walking Toby down the middle of the street, he turned in at the hotel, tied Toby off, and went inside to get a room for the night.

Across the street, Morgan Baxter rubbed at his whiskers and pondered his next move. He'd been so sure that Sheriff Big Al Dolan would be able to handle the bounty hunter that he hadn't bothered to come up with an alternate plan. One thing was for sure. Whatever that plan was, it was going to take more than one man.

By late that afternoon the mayor and two members of the town council had met with J.T. and told him that Sheriff Dolan's actions had been taken on his own. In their opinion, J.T. had clearly acted in self-defense. The town wanted no trouble, and as a show of their good faith, Dolan had been fired as sheriff. No replacement had been appointed yet. It seemed that for the time being no one wanted the job, even at twice the normal pay. When J.T. had inquired as to the whereabouts of the Baxters, he got the answer he'd expected. They didn't know. Their cooperation only went so far. They wouldn't interfere in J.T.'s business, but by the same token, they wouldn't do anything to help him either. The mayor was quick to point out that the Baxters did have friends in Steeles Grove and that neither the council nor the town could be held responsible for what those friends might do.

J.T. assured the mayor that he had no intention of turning their town into a shooting gallery where innocent people might be hurt. He intended to leave in the morning, but until then, any influence they had with the townspeople would go a long way toward preventing trouble. His only interest was the Baxters.

The three men had left his room feeling confident that they could keep a handle on the situation, at least for the next twenty-four hours. From his hotel window, J.T. had watched the trio confer in the middle of the street for a few minutes, then split up and move from store to store. He could only imagine what they were telling the townspeople, but it was a good bet the fact that he would be leaving in the morning was at the top of their list.

In a town the size of Steeles Grove, men like the Baxters were certain to have made a few enemies. J.T. was betting that sooner or later someone with a grudge against the brothers would contact him with information about where they were. As afternoon slipped into night, J.T. sat in his room playing solitaire and waited.

He didn't have to wait long. An hour after dark there was a knock on his door. With his gun drawn, J.T. stood to the side of the door. He opened it to find a rough-looking man with a patch over his left eye standing there with his hands raised.

"Don't shoot. I ain't armed. Just come to talk."

J.T. motioned the man into the room, noting that the man was wearing an empty holster. A quick check of the hallway before closing the door convinced J.T. that the man was alone. Lowering his gun, J.T. asked, "Who are you, mister?"

"Name's Lee Howard. I was just over to Reily's Saloon. Thought you oughta know, Ol' Man Baxter's offerin' a thousand dollars to anybody that'll gun you down."

"Where's he at now?"

"Still at Reily's, I reckon. He's drunk as hell. I was on my way outta town. Just thought somebody oughta warn you."

"Any idea where his boys are?"

"Nope. They were here four or five days ago. Spent

one night, then rode out. But they'll be back, you can count on that. They got this town buffaloed. Ain't nobody got the guts to stand up to them and their old man."

The first rule of being a bounty hunter was to be suspicious of everybody and trust no one. That was especially true of the Baxters, who had already shown how low they could go by their actions in Nacogdoches. It was understandable that J.T. would be leery of anyone in this town who offered him help of any kind. Watching the man's eyes, he asked, "Why are you telling me this?"

The man smiled. "Let's just say we had mutual acquaintances up in Missouri during the war and let it go at that."

J.T. studied the man's face, trying to place it from among the hundreds he'd seen during the war.

"Don't trouble yourself, Cap'in. I was just one of the boys back then, but I sure remember you, all right. Recall you knockin' eight Yankees outta their saddles while your horse was ridin' at full stride during that battle outside Centralia. Damnest shootin' I ever saw."

J.T. holstered his gun. This man wasn't a threat; he was a fellow comrade in arms from the past. The only way he could have known J.T. was a captain at that time was to have been there himself.

J.T. extended his hand to the man. "Thanks for the information. Can I buy you a drink?"

Howard shook hands as he replied, "Wish I could, Cap'in, but I got me a job lined up as ramrod for a herd pushin' north in the mornin'. Gotta be headin' out, but I sure appreciate the offer. Maybe next time."

"Fair enough. Come on, I'll walk down with you."

The two men headed downstairs and out in front of the hotel. Howard shook hands one more time, then swung himself up in the saddle.

"Cap'in. You watch out for that Ol' Man Baxter. He's

a mean son of a bitch. He'll backshoot you if he gets the chance."

"I'll do that, Mr. Howard. Thanks again, and good luck to you."

"You too, Cap'in."

J.T. watched the only friend he had in this town ride off into the darkness. It was strange how the past always seemed to be crossing with the present. Cole Younger the day before, now Lee Howard. As he walked toward Reily's saloon, J.T. wondered when and where the past and present would cross paths again.

There was a loud and rowdy crowd in attendance at Reily's place. But then that was understandable. At Reily's a man got a fair deal at the tables and honest-to-God real whiskey from the bottle, not that watered-down cow piss everyone else served.

J.T. walked through the doors, and hadn't gone ten feet when suddenly the place went quiet as a tomb. All except for one loudmouthed older man with a face full of whiskers at the far end of the bar, who was ranting and raving about the law and bounty hunters. J.T. stepped up to the bar. Immediately a number of the patrons began leaving by the front and side exits of the saloon. Sean Reily, the owner, watched the mass exodus. Setting a bottle and a glass on the bar in front of J.T., he introduced himself.

"Name's Sean Reily, Mr. Law. I own the place. Now don't be takin' it personal, but I'm hopin' you won't be stayin' long. Sure as your very presence has done cost me at least fifty dollars."

J.T. poured himself a drink. "Don't worry, Reily. I drink a lot."

Someone at the end of the bar had finally gotten Morgan Baxter to shut up long enough to notice J.T. standing at the bar. The place was still quiet as a church. Everyone knew there was going to be trouble, especially Reily.

"Now look here, you two," Reily said. "We won't be wantin' to see trouble in here now. I'd be appreciatin' it if you'd be so kind as to take any gentlemanly disagreements outside."

J.T. turned at the bar and faced Morgan Baxter, who stood at the end of the bar thirty feet away.

"Not going to be any trouble, is there, Baxter?" said J.T.

For a second Morgan Baxter considered going for his gun, but even drunk as he was, he knew better. This bounty man would have six bullets in him before he could clear leather. No, thought the old man, there wasn't going to be any gunplay tonight. But J.T. Law was going to have plenty come morning. He'd already seen to that piece of business. Weaving back and forth, Baxter grabbed the bar to steady himself, then yelled to Reily.

"Ain't gonna be no trouble. Not from me nohow. You might wanta tell that scum-suckin' sonofabitch down there that."

Baxter raised his hand to point at J.T. and almost lost his balance. Quickly grabbing the bar again, to keep from falling on his face, he continued with the insults.

"Goddamn, low-life, bounty-huntin' bastard. That's what ya are, ain't it? A damn hired gun for the state of Texas."

J.T. poured himself another drink, as if totally ignoring the drunken remarks. This seem to infuriate the old man even more.

"Come on, bounty man! Here I am! Why don't ya start shootin'? Hell, that's how ya got that reputation of yers, ain't it. Shootin' drunks?"

Everyone in the place kept waiting for J.T. to do something. He'd already shown more patience than most of them would have in dealing with this loudmouthed old bastard.

"Ya just keep hangin' round, bounty man. My boys'll be gettin' back here soon. An when they do, they'll put so many holes in your ass your own maw wouldn't know ya. Yes, sir. Just like they did them no-good Rangers up in Nacogdoches."

Morgan Baxter had just crossed the line. Slamming his glass down on the bar, J.T. began walking toward the old man.

"He's drunk, Mr. Law," said Reily.

"Well, I'm not!" came the reply.

A look of fear came over Baxter's face as J.T. closed the distance between them. Standing less than two feet away, the bounty man stared Baxter right in the eye. Fear could work wonders on people, especially drunks.

"I . . . I ain't drawin' on ya, ya hear?" With his hands shaking, Baxter quickly unbuckled his gunbelt and let it fall to the floor.

"Y'all see it! I ain't heeled! Ya gun me now, it'll be murder. I ain't heeled, gawddammit."

J.T. leaned forward only inches from the man's face.

"You scared, old man?" whispered J.T. "Well, you should be. I'm going to see to it that every one of your sons hang for what they've done. If I had my way, you'd swing right along with 'em, you loudmouth son of a bitch."

Baxter suddenly went for a knife he had hidden under his shirt. Before he could pull it, J.T. drew his pistol and brought it down on top of Morgan Baxter's head. The old man dropped like a poleaxed steer. Pulling the knife from the man's shirt, J.T. tossed it on the bar for everyone to see. He then reached into Baxter's vest pocket and pulling out a wad of money, placed it on the bar in front of Reily.

"That should cover some of the business you lost, Reily."

Looking around the bar, J.T. spoke in a loud and clear voice.

"Any you boys thinking about collecting that thousand dollars this old fool's been offering—I'd advise against it. I'm here for the Baxter brothers. I got no fight with anyone else in this town. But if you're inclined to try your luck, I'm staying at the hotel across the street." That said, J.T. left the saloon and returned to his hotel room.

Sean Reily told some of the men to get Morgan over to the doc's office. There was blood all over the floor from a three-inch gash in the middle of his head. He was going to need some sewing up. As they were carrying the man out, one of the men at the bar muttered, "Damn bounty man. He'd didn't have to go an' pistol ol' Morgan like that."

Folding the money from the bar and placing it in his shirt pocket, Reily stared out the doors at the man entering the hotel as he said, "Right you are, lad. He sure should have killed the bastard—I would've."

SEVEN

THE MORNING SUN broke through the hotel window and woke J.T. from what had been a restless night's sleep. A chair had been propped against the door and a large chest of drawers moved in front of the window. He woke more tired than when he had gone to bed. Knowing that he had to stay alert for the slightest sound that might signal an attempt to enter his room, he had never really gone into a sound sleep.

He hated nights like that, but a thousand dollars was a lot of money, and the temptation to try to collect it had to be a strong one among a number of the townspeople. But after all his precautions and his loss of sleep, nothing had happened during the night. He already missed the peace and quiet of the Manor House.

Finally up and moving about, he packed his belongings and wondered how Morgan Baxter was feeling this morning. Between too much liquor and the crack on the head, the old man had to have one hell of a headache. But then he'd brought it all on himself. He should have known when to shut up, but most drunks never did.

With his saddlebags over his shoulder, J.T. took the key to the room, closed the door, and headed down to the desk. The old man had blurted out something about his boys getting "back here soon." There was no way of knowing if that was just whiskey talk or if the Baxter brothers had returned during the night. Either way, J.T. had to be ready for anything.

Tossing the key to the clerk at the desk, he asked. "You fellas remember to have my horse saddled and ready this morning?"

"Yes, sir. Boy tied him off out front a few minutes ago."

Thanking the man, J.T. walked into the cool morning air. The streets were empty. Toby stood at the rail. He shook his mane and pawed at the ground with one hoof at the sight of his owner. Throwing the saddlebags on behind his saddle and tying them down, J.T. fished around in his coat pocket and brought out some sugar for Toby. The buckskin snatched it gently from J.T.'s hand.

"Well, Toby. Looks like that ol' man was all whiskey talk."

Toby suddenly jerked his head up and began to prance around nervously.

"Whoa, fellow. What's the matter with you? Somethin' got you spooked?"

"Hey! Bounty man! Turn around!"

The booming words seemed to echo down the empty street. J.T. turned to find three cowboys standing in the middle of the street. They were spread out in a line, with a distance of ten to fifteen feet between them. Their feet were set and their hands poised next to their guns. The big man in the center who had called to him was apparently the leader and spokesman for the trio.

"Looks like the tables are turned, bounty man. This mornin' it's you that's worth a thousand dollars. Kinda funny, don't you think?"

In the few seconds the man was talking, J.T. had already summed up his situation. The spokesman was the oldest, with the two outside men maybe in their mid-to-late twenties. The kid on the right was carrying a Smith & Wesson Schofield, but his holster was hitched too high to give him any speed with the long-barreled weapon, and his feet were too far apart.

The man on the left carried a Colt .44, the holster slightly forward and resting on the front part of his leg. But it wasn't tied down. When he attempted to draw, the holster would rise up and away from his leg, costing him precious seconds before the gun would clear the holster. His feet were too close together.

It was the older cowboy who was the real threat. He wore a Colt Peacemaker housed in black leather. The holster had a slight shine to it, meaning that it had been oiled down and hand-rubbed, inside and out, to give the pistol a smooth motion coming out of the oil-slick leather. The holster hung midway and slightly to the rear. This man practiced a lot, and knew where that holster had to be to give him the best angle and advantage. His feet were spread exactly the width of his shoulders. This man might be working as a cowboy now, but the rig he was wearing and the gunfighter stance were testimony to another past.

J.T. eased the side of his coat back and with his thumb, pushed a portion of the material into the back of his gun-belt to keep it clear of the holster. Across the street, three horses were tied off in front of the general store. J.T. noticed that they bore the Box T brand. One of the largest ranches in the area. There was no doubt in his mind that these three horses belonged to the cowboys.

Money could influence a man faster than anything else.

It caused men to take risks that they normally wouldn't even think twice about. Nobody knew this better than John Thomas Law. He'd fallen victim to that very influence himself following the war. The lack of money and the poor judgment because of it were reasons why he avoided Kansas and Missouri at all costs. In some sheriff or marshal's office there was a flyer with his description. Oh, yes, J.T. knew better than most the mistakes a man could make in life, all due to the lure of easy money.

"Now you boys oughta think this thing over. I see by those horses you're cowboys that ride for the Box T. Been more than a few good men lost their lives over fast money and bad decisions. You're cowboys, not gunmen. That's somethin' to think about."

The young man on the right spoke up. "We thought about it all night, bounty man. A thousand dollars is a powerful lot of money for cowhands. Means not havin' to winter in this shithole, an' no ridin' line, freezin' our asses off for a bunch of dumb cows. Oh, we've thought about it, all right."

"How's it feel, bounty man?" asked the man on the left. "How's it feel havin' a price on your head for a change?"

The truth be known, J.T. didn't think about it either way. He'd already accepted the fact this profession would get him killed. Either on some street like this or in some saloon or alleyway. So what was there to be afraid of?

"It don't bother me in the least, son. We're all gonna die sooner or later. A lucky few get to pick the time and place. But you know what does bother me?"

"What's that?"

"The fact that I'm gonna have to kill all three of you, an' I don't get a damn dollar for any one of you."

"That's mighty big talk for a man facin' three-to-one odds, mister," said the middle man.

"You forget, friend. I do this for a living. Now, I'm

gonna ask you one more time. Let this thing go, get on those horses, and ride back to the Box T. I got no fight with you boys, an' I sure as hell don't want to have to kill you."

J.T. noticed the young man on the right waver a bit. He saw the look in the man's eyes. He wanted to run for that horse and get as far away from here as he could. But J.T. knew no matter how strong the urge, he wouldn't do it. The shame of having run away would kill him a thousand times, while J.T. could only kill him once.

"How you wanta play this?" asked the oldest.

"It's your party, friend," said J.T. "You start the ball."

J.T. fixed his attention on the oldest man, figuring that he would be the fastest and the most likely to draw first. He was right.

The man blinked just before his hand came up, his thumb cocking the Peacemaker as it was coming out of the holster. The wrist arched as the barrel began to come up, but that was as far as it went.

J.T.'s first shot shattered the man's wrist, sending the Colt tumbling into the dirt. His second shot tore through the man's right leg, just above the knee. The middle man cried out in pain, spun around twice, and crumpled into the dirt holding his leg with his good hand.

The kid on the right was still struggling to get the Schofield out of the holster when a .45 slug ripped through his shoulder and knocked him backward and flat on his back in the street.

The young cowboy on the left had his .44 out, but his hand was shaking so badly that when he fired, the bullet hit a washtub hanging from a nail fifteen feet to J.T.'s right. The sight of his friends shot and bleeding and the gunfighter dropping to one knee and bringing the barrel of his .45 to bear on him was more than he could handle. His wrist went limp and the .44 fell to the ground. Shaking all over and with his eyes closed, the cowboy yelled out, "Go ahead, dammit. Do it! I got it comin'!"

Lowing his gun, J.T. stood up. "Not today, kid. Go help your friends."

The cowboy's eyes slowly opened, followed by a grateful sigh. He suddenly looked as if the weight of the world had just been lifted off his shoulders, and he ran to help his young friend who had been shot in the shoulder.

J.T., meanwhile, walked over to the middle man, who was now sitting up. Blood dripped from the shattered wrist and covered his wounded leg. As J.T. knelt down next to him, he saw the pain written all over his face.

"Hurt?" J.T. asked.

"Well, hell, yes, it hurts!"

"Good! You're the oldest of this bunch. You should've known better. What's your name?"

"Tom . . . Tom Lowery."

J.T. shook his head. "No, I mean your real name."

The man lowered his head and muttered, "Trace. Trace McCuthin."

J.T. knew the man was more than just a simple cowboy by the way he had faced off against him in the street.

"Gunfighter out of Arizona, right? I thought you were dead. Killed by some *federales* down in Mexico. Four, five years ago."

The man forced a smile as he looked over at J.T. "They damn near got it done too. Took four bullets, but managed to pull through it and get back to Texas. Figured everybody thinkin' I was dead would give me a good chance to get outta the business. Got tired of sleepin' with one eye open all the time and havin' to worry about every gun-happy kid that come along lookin' to make a reputation. Changed my name and found me a good job with the Box T here. Gonna make foreman 'fore long. Work's damn hard, but it's honest."

"Well, what was all this about? Hell, you should have known these boys wouldn't stand a chance up against a professional. Even you, for that matter. I could have killed all three of you."

"Hell, yes, I knew that. I haven't wore this shootin' rig since that business in Mexico. But I didn't have a lot of choice. Morgan Baxter somehow found out who I was. Said he'd get me fired from the T and spread the word all over that Trace McCuthin was still alive. So you see, I'd be right back where I started. Only way out was to try and take you. Meant to go it alone, but the boys here found me oilin' down my rig. We've rode a lot of fence together an' they were comin' with me. They wouldn't have it any other way. They're young, but good pals."

"They know who you really are?"

McCuthin shook his head from side to side. "Naw. Reckon I should have told 'em, but I figured the fewer people that knew the better. Right now that's just you an Ol' Man Baxter."

The shooting had brought a crowd of people who were moving up the street toward the men on the ground. J.T. figured this was a good time to leave.

"You going to be all right?" he asked.

"Yeah. Doc'll be busy for a while, but least we ain't dead." Nodding toward his wrist, McCuthin continued. "Looks like you put an end to my gunfightin' days for good. But figurin' you could've killed us, it's a small price to pay."

The crowd was drawing closer.

"Reckon I better ride," said J.T. "I done crippled up the sheriff, cracked Ol Man Baxter's head, and now shot two boys from the biggest ranch in the county. I don't think these folks are going to put up with me being around any longer. You don't worry about Baxter or his boys. I'll take care of that business."

Moving quickly to his horse, J.T. mounted and walked Toby over to the two young cowboys. Looking down at them, he said, "You boys listen to Mr. Lowery next time and you might live to an old age."

Glancing over at McCuthin, he touched the tip of his hat as he said, "See you around, Mr. Lowery."

The local populace gathered round the wounded men and asked what had happened. McCuthin told them it was a misunderstanding that had gotten out of hand.

Sean Reily watched the bounty man ride away and shook his head. He'd been in this country nearly ten years and he still had a hard time understanding people like J.T. Law. The man was supposed to be some kind of hardcase killer, yet he'd put up with Old Man Baxter's foul-mouthed slander and only dealt him a crack on the head. Now three men brace him for the thousand dollars on his head and he doesn't kill a one of them. So just where was the bloodthirsty killer everyone talked about? Reily couldn't figure it out.

But then he wasn't alone. J.T. Law was a complicated man. Nobody really knew him, his past, or what motivated him to take the risks he took on a daily basis. When it came right down to it, John Thomas Law was a loner. He had no close friends and he wanted to keep it that way.

EIGHT

J.T. HAD DONE some checking around and found out that the Baxter spread was located in the Santa Rosa Valley, ten miles south of Steeles Grove. Now perched on a ledge that afforded him a view of the entire Baxter ranch, he watched and waited. If he was right, it wouldn't be long before the old man got word that the morning's activities in the street had not gone well. J.T. figured if he was as mean and hot-tempered sober as he was drunk, his reaction to the news should be quite a show.

He had just finished his cigar when he saw dust rising from the north. Sure enough, it was a rider from town, and he was burning up the road to the Baxter ranch. Down by the main gate, someone yelled back toward the house that there was a rider coming. Morgan Baxter came busting out the front door, off the porch, and almost ran to the gate. The old man was easy to spot. The entire top of his head was wrapped in bandages.

The rider pulled back on the reins and shot out of the

saddle, hitting the ground at a run. Two cowboys grabbed him before he could pile into the gate. J.T. couldn't hear what they were saying from that far away, but he really didn't have to. Their body movements told him all he needed to know.

Suddenly, the old man knocked the rider down and kicked him a wicked blow in the side. J.T. didn't need to guess what he was saying; he could hear the old man yelling at the top of his voice.

"Goddamn! Sonofabitch!" The words echoed through the hills. Baxter kept right on screaming and yelling as he pulled the bandages from his head.

'Ya should've shot the sonofabitch when ya had the chance! Idiots! I'm surrounded by goddamn idiots! Pete, get my horse. Rest of ya get yer rifles an' move up in them rocks round the ranch. He shows his ass around here while I'm gone, ya kill the bastard! A thousand dollars to the man that drops him. Ya hear me? A thousand dollars cash!"

Morgan Baxter had calmed down by the time the man called Pete had brought him his horse. The two men conferred for a few minutes; then Baxter mounted and rode off to the north. That was just what J.T. had been waiting for. The old man was going to warn his boys. He'd lead J.T. straight to them.

Morgan Baxter circled wide around Steeles Grove, and rode due north toward the Nehes River. Once there, he turned west, riding along the riverbank until he came to a place called Boone's Ferry. It wasn't much. A small way station with a plank-board saloon, a general store, a blacksmith shop, a livery, and a whorehouse.

J.T. pulled up short of the station. Keeping the small cluster of buildings in sight, he eased Toby along the ridge and into a stand of trees. He watched Morgan Baxter go straight to the saloon. It was then that he noticed the old man's horse was the only one saddled and tied in front of any of the buildings. Locating the stable, he counted nine horses in the corral. J.T. was certain now that four of those horses belonged to the Baxter brothers. But what about the other five? As it stood now, counting the old man, J.T. would be going up against five men. Pretty long odds for sure, but if any of those other horses belonged to friends of the Baxters, those slim odds got even worse.

Stepping down, J.T. undid the cinch on his saddle.

"Well, Toby. Looks like we got 'em where we want 'em. Question is, what d' we do with 'em now?"

A short, chubby fellow with a tattered undershirt came out of the bar and ran across the square to the whorehouse. A few minutes later, four men came out of the house, tucking in their shirts and walking fast in the direction of the saloon. It was the Baxter boys.

"Seems Papa Baxter's called a family meetin'. Now if we're lucky, an' them boys don't get jackrabbit fever, they'll stay put for the night. That's when we'll go for 'em, Toby. After dark."

Inside the bar, Morgan Baxter was swigging down whiskey from a bottle as he waited for his boys. His head hurt like hell. Of course, he had no way of knowing that the doc had been close to falling-down drunk himself when they had carried Baxter into his office. The sawbones had sewn the stitches too far apart and too tight. That was a big part of why his head was throbbing like a bass drum.

Nate and Charlie came through the door, followed closely by Tom and Coe. They passed by the bar, grabbing glasses and another bottle, then headed to where their father was sitting. Pulling up a chair, Nate was the first to notice the ugly gash in the top of his father's head.

"Damn, Pa! What happen to you?"

The other boys rose halfway out of their chairs to have a look at the bloody wound.

"Sonofabitch pistol-whipped me at Reily's last night."

"What!" shouted Nate. "Tell us who it was, Pa. The bastard'll be dead before sundown."

The other boys joined in. "Yeah, Pa. Who was it?" asked Tom.

Charlie barked, "We'll weight the sonofabitch down with lead."

The old man lowered the bottle. "Well, if ya can do that, y'all be the first. There's fourteen dead men in the ground right now thought the same thing."

They suddenly fell silent, each looking around at the others.

Morgan Baxter laughed. "What's the matter, boys? Ya thinkin' some timid-ass store clerk could do this to your pa and still be walking around? Hell, no, they wouldn't. Same fella that give me this knocked the balls off Big Al Dolan and took a damn shotgun away from him. This mornin' that same fella faced off against three men in a gunfight. He wounded two of 'em an' scared the shit out of the third one. But he could've killed all three of 'em if he'd had a mind to. So now tell me again how yer gonna take up for yer dear ol' pa."

The boys were momentarily stunned by their pa's story. Tom leaned back in his chair and muttered, "Jesus. He disarmed Al Dolan, an' with him carryin' a damn shotgun. Hell, I wouldn't even try that, an' he's a friend of ours."

Charlie quickly agreed. "No shit. An' goin' up against three guns. Man's gotta be out of his head, buckin' them kind of odds."

"That—or damn good at what he does," said Nate. "Gunman or bounty hunter, Pa?" he asked.

The old man leaned forward. "Ya see that? That's why

Nate runs this outfit. He takes the time to think things through."

"Which is it, Pa?"

"Both," he replied.

There was another moment of silence around the table as the brothers once again looked at one another, each trying to figure out who this mystery man might be. But it was Nate who figured it out.

"Damn! John Thomas Law. Sonofabitch went up against four guns in Waco last winter. Killed all four and walked away without a scratch."

The old man laughed, then took another pull on the bottle before he said, "Ya boys wanted to be famous. Reckon ya made it. J.T. Law don't go chasin' after just anybody. He goes after the big boys. The ones worth the big payday. Now what ya gonna do?"

Coe Baxter didn't care what the others thought. Any man who could stand up to four guns and walk away was a man to stay clear of, and he let it be known how he felt about it.

"Hell, what are we waitin' for. Let's get saddled an' out of here before he heads our way."

Tom didn't say anything, but one look at his face told the others that he felt the same way Coe did. Charlie, on the other hand, was staying quiet. Waiting for Nate to make the call.

"J.T. Law. I'll be damned," said Nate with a grin. "Those goddamn Rangers couldn't get the job done, so they go out an' hire this bastard an' send him after us. Well, we ain't runnin', boys. Not from no damn bounty hunter. Don't care if it is J.T. Law. We'll send his ass to hell just like we did those two Rangers."

"I'm with you, brother," said Charlie. "We take down J.T. Law, won't be nobody in Texas don't know our names."

While the others began drinking and bragging about what they'd do to this bounty hunter, Coe Baxter sat back in his chair and tried to shake a feeling of impending doom.

Nate Baxter's attitude was just what the man waiting in the trees had counted on. Come nightfall, the bounty man would make his move.

A FULL MOON was rising as J.T. made his way slowly down a slope and into position behind the blacksmith's shop. From there he could see the front entrance to the saloon and the whorehouse across the way. Just before dark he had watched the old man and three of his boys leave the saloon and head for the whorehouse. They were still there. He didn't know which Baxter was still in the saloon, but it really didn't matter. He intended to have them all before the night was over.

Moving like a cat through the shadows, J.T. went around to the rear of the saloon. Easing himself up to a windowsill, he peered inside. The bartender was busy washing glasses. A big man sat with one of the girls from across the way. Judging by his size of his arms, J.T. figured him for the blacksmith. The only other person in the room was a young cowboy sitting at a table near the front door. According to the descriptions he had of the group, this had to be Coe Baxter.

Circling back around to the front of the building, J.T. quietly moved up onto the porch. Drawing his Peacemaker with one hand, he reached out with the other and turned down the lamp that hung on a corner post. He didn't turn it all the way out, but rather just low enough so that anyone looking toward the saloon would have a hard time seeing anyone on that side of the porch. He kept inching his way forward toward the swinging doors.

Every few steps he would glance over at the whorehouse, just in case someone came walking out and headed for the saloon.

Coe sat at a table in the saloon across from the doors. He had a bottle and a glass in front of him, but he hadn't been drinking that much. His thoughts were on the bounty man who he knew would be riding their way. Why couldn't Nate listen to Coe, just this once? It was stupid to be drinking and whoring at a time like this. There was a man coming to kill them, or worse, take them back for hanging, and Coe seemed to be the only one taking it seriously. If he had any sense at all he'd be over in that corral right now, saddling his horse and heading to Mexico. But then like his pa had always said, he wasn't very smart.

Having inched his way to the swinging doors, J.T. slowly pressed the right one open and brought his .45 up, pointing it directly at the young cowboy's head. Coe hadn't noticed anything at first. It wasn't until he brought his glass up to take a drink that he saw the man standing in the shadows next to the doorway and the gun in his hand that was pointed straight at him.

J.T. brought a finger up to his lips, warning the boy to stay quiet. He then moved the barrel of the gun up and down, motioning for him to stand up. Coe Baxter wasn't about to argue with a .45 being held by a man who had already killed fourteen men, according to Pa. Placing his glass down, he slowly slid his chair back and stood up. J.T. motioned for him to come outside. Coe Baxter followed instructions well. As he reached the doors, the bartender looked up and saw him leaving.

"Hey, Coe. You gonna get you some of that hog farm excitement, are you? You gonna be comin' back?"

Coe didn't answer or bother to look the man's way as he walked out the doors.

"Okay, then. I guess I'll be seein' you later," said the barkeep as he went back to wiping the stack of glasses in front of him.

Once he had the boy outside, J.T. grabbed a fistful of shirt and pulled the kid off the porch and back behind the blacksmith shop. Pushing him hard up against the wall, he placed the barrel of the cocked .45 firmly against the boy's forehead.

"Now I'm not gonna have any trouble out of you, am I, boy?"

Coe Baxter's eyes were as big as silver dollars, and J.T. could feel him trembling all over.

"No. No, sir. Can't say the same for my brothers."

"You let me worry about that. Now turn around."

Coe did as he was told. Not knowing what to expect, he gave a sigh of relief when he felt a pair of irons being locked firmly around his wrists. Moving him to a corner of the corral, J.T. tied him to a post, then fastened a gag tightly around his mouth.

"You behave yourself, kid, an' you just might live through this night."

J.T. disappeared into the darkness again, this time moving up to the back of the whorehouse. It was an old wooden two-story affair that had seen better days. There was a rickety set of stairs that led up to a side door on the second floor. But he quickly ruled out the back stairs after taking only two steps. They creaked so loudly that any attempt to climb them and keep quiet was out of the question. He would have to figure another way.

Quietly, he went to the side of the building. Finding a lit window, he knelt down and slowly eased the window up an inch. He listened for any sound of movement or breathing coming from inside. The room was empty. Bringing the window the rest of the way up, he climbed into the room. Finding his way to the door, he opened it slightly and peered out into the hallway. There was no one there, but he could hear loud voices and laughter coming from a large parlor located just beyond the staircase. Judging from the sounds, and different voices, there were two men and either two or three women in the parlor.

The problem was, were they the Baxters? There were still nine horses in that corral. Only four belonged to the boys he was after. Did the others belong to friends of the Baxters or just some cowboys passing through? The problem was solved a few minutes later when a woman came down the stairs and stopped a few feet from the room where J.T. was hiding. In a high-pitched voice, she yelled into the parlor.

"Hey, Frank! You an' Bert want somethin' to eat?"

A tall, lanky fella, wearing nothing but a pair of longhandle pants and a smile, stepped out into the hallway.

"Hell, yeah, Marty. You got any beefsteak and eggs?"

"Anything you want, honey. Might even stir up some biscuits an' gravy if you'll behave yourself."

"Come on, Bert. Marty's gonna cook us up steak an' eggs."

The entire bunch from the parlor, two men and three women, followed Marty down the hallway and into the kitchen. Now was his chance.

J.T. opened the door all the way and stepped out into the hallway. For the moment this part of the house was quiet. All the talking and laughter came from the kitchen, located somewhere at the back of the house. Stepping past the staircase to the parlor entrance, he made a quick survey of the layout. The parlor was empty; beyond it there were three more doors. Two were standing open. More than likely these belonged to Frank and Bert. Moving light on his feet, J.T. stepped up to the third room and put his ear to the door. He heard a woman's voice inside.

"Oh, come on, Willy. I know ya can ride this pony one

more time. I just know ya can. Here, let me help ya wake that thing up."

J.T. couldn't help but crack a smile. He gave a sigh of relief as well. At least three of those horses belonged to these cowboys out for a night of fun and relaxation. It was reasonable to assume that the other two belonged to a couple of local residents. Better yet, that meant that the Baxters were all staying on the second floor.

Moving back to the staircase, J.T. drew his gun and cocked the hammer back. Staying close to the wall, he began making his way up the staircase. He was midway up the stairs when he heard a door open below. In an instant J.T. realized he had made a mistake. There had been another room next to the one he'd come out of. He had missed it on his way out, and in his haste to corner the Baxters upstairs, he'd neglected to check for it. That one single mistake was about to blow his plan all to pieces.

J.T. looked back down the stairs at the same instant Old Man Baxter looked up. For a fleeting second their eyes met, then all hell broke loose. Morgan Baxter had come out of the room with his gunbelt slung over his shoulder. The moment he saw J.T. he made a desperate grab for his pistol, but even in his own mind, he had to know he didn't have a chance. Three shots rang out from the Colt in J.T.'s hand. All three hit Morgan Baxter dead center in the chest, the impact blowing him back into the room he'd walked out of only seconds ago. A loud scream came from inside the room. A second later, a naked woman came running out into the hallway screaming, "Murder! Murder!"

"Aw, goddamnit!" shouted J.T. as he started taking the stairs two at a time in an effort to reach the second-floor landing before the other Baxters could get out of their rooms. He was four steps too late.

At the sound of the first shot, Nate had bolted from the bed and with gun in hand, run out into the hallway. Catching sight of J.T. near the head of the stairs, he cut loose with four hurried shots that tore holes in the wall only inches above the bounty man's head. J.T. fired three quick rounds that drove Nate back against the wall.

"Charlie! Tom! Come a-runnin' boys! We got company!" shouted Nate.

Charlie jumped off the woman he'd been riding, and grabbing his gunbelt, swung the door to his room open. Pulling his gun from the holster, he dashed out into the hallway. Out of the corner of his eye he saw a figure dart out of a dark room. He turned and fired. The girl screamed and grabbing her stomach, doubled over, falling to the floor. Tom Baxter had pushed her out the door ahead of him.

"Dammit, Charlie, he's down here!" yelled Nate.

Charlie looked down at the girl and cussing under his breath, ran to join his brother.

Tom stepped over the body of the young woman twisting and moaning in pain on the floor. Glancing down at her, he uttered, "Sorry, kid. But better you than me."

Joining his two brothers against the wall, Tom asked, "How many are they?"

"Just saw one. If it's J.T. Law, he'll be alone. He don't work with nobody else."

"Where's Pa?" asked Charlie.

"Dead, more'n likely. Figure that was them three shots we heard," said Nate.

"He still on the stairs?"

Nate looked over at Tom. "How the hell do I know. Ya wanta stick your head down there an' find out?"

"Hell, no. Not me!"

Seeing the side door that led to the outside stairs, Nate turned to Charlie.

"You two go out and down the back way, then come in the front. We'll trap him on the stairs an' get him in a cross fire."

Charlie grinned at Nate's idea. He grabbed Tom and the two ran down the hallway, past the girl who now lay in a pool of blood on the floor. She wasn't moving any-more. She was dead. Jerking the side door open, Charlie quickly checked to make sure it was clear. Then he and Tom headed down the rickety stairs and raced around to the front of the building. Kicking the front door open, they dashed inside, their guns pointed at the staircase. But there was no one there. J.T. was gone.

"Nate! He's on the move. The stairs are clear. Come on down."

Nate hurried down the stairs to join his brothers. As he did, Tom glanced into the room near the staircase. Calling his brothers over, he pointed to the body of their father.

"You were right, Nate. Pa must of stumbled upon him while he was headed up the stairs."

There was no emotion in Charlie's voice as he replied, "The old sonofabitch won't be beatin' nobody else with no razor straps."

Tom was the only one who seemed to feel any remorse. "He killed our pa, the no-good bastard."

"Yeah, saved me the trouble," said Nate. "We'll have to split up. Search the house first, then move outside. Any-body seen Coe?"

"Not since we left the bar," said Tom, still staring at the bloody, lifeless form of their father.

"Tom, you go back upstairs an' check all the rooms. He coulda slipped up there somehow. Charlie, you an' me'll check out the rooms down here. Let's go," ordered Nate.

After the exchange of gunfire with Nate, J.T. had hur-ried back down the stairs just in time to intercept the group coming down the hallway from the kitchen. He had forced them all back into the kitchen. All told, there were the two cowboys and five women, among them the madam who owned the place. She was a heavyset, hard-looking old gal who had been in the business a long time and had no problem speaking her mind.

"Hey, asshole! Quit shakin' that damn shooter in my face an' tell us what the hell's going on out there."

J.T. admired a woman who didn't mince words.

"You folks gotta get out of here. The shootin's not over yet, and these Baxter boys ain't particular about who gets shot here tonight. You can make it to the woods behind the blacksmith shop an' lay low till this thing's over."

"But what about our partner Willy? He's in one of them rooms down there," said one of the cowboys.

"Didn't see him or the girl he was with when I came back. Door to his room was open. I figure they done high-tailed it out the window. Probably already hidin' in the woods. Come on, you don't have much time."

Kicking the back door open, J.T. stepped out and checked to see that it was clear, then yelled, "Come on. Get out of there."

As the others ran out the door and off the porch, the madam hesitated. "Who the hell's gonna pay for the damages to my place?"

J.T. looked at her and shook his head. "Damn, lady. I don't think I'd be worryin' about that right now."

There was the sudden sound of voices coming down the hall.

"Well, hell, no, you wouldn't. It ain't your place that's bein' shot all to—"

Before she could finish, J.T. threw his arms around the big woman and pushed with all his might, his momentum carrying them both out the door only seconds before Nate and Charlie burst into the kitchen, firing wildly in all directions. Three bullets ripped apart the door frame where the woman had been standing.

J.T.'s actions had sent the couple flying off the porch onto the hard ground. The fall had knocked the madam unconscious. J.T. struggled to get himself untangled from the woman, but he had taken the brunt of the fall, her weight taking the air out of him and sending his Peacemaker flying out of his hand and into the dirt fifteen feet away. By the time he could breath again and work himself free, he looked up to find Nate and Charlie standing on the porch, their guns pointed at him and big grins on both their faces. They had him and they knew it. So did the bounty man. There was still the Colt in the shoulder rig, but he was down on all fours in the dirt and he knew he'd never make the grab before they shot him all to hell. He was good, but nobody was that good. All he could do now was wait for them to end it.

With his gun pointed straight at J.T.'s head, Nate laughed.

"Wanta thank you for killin' that ol' man in there, bounty man. Been wantin' to do it for years. Just never could screw up the nerve to get her done."

"Ya ain't so all damn much now, are ya, Mr. J.T. Law," said Charlie, "Hell, ya look like a bitch dog all hunkered down like that, don't he, Nate? Don't he remind ya of a bitch dog? All bent over there an' ready for a hard bone."

Both brothers laughed. They were loving this and didn't want to rush their fun. But J.T. had had enough.

"You ignorant sonsabitches's gonna shoot or just try an' talk me to death?"

"Let him have it, Charlie," said Nate.

Both men pulled the triggers on their pistols at the same time, but there wasn't the exploding sound of gunfire they had expected. Only the dull "click" of the hammers as they fell on empty chambers. The boys had used up their six shots shooting up the kitchen, but in the excitement of seeing their prey rolling around on the ground with the fat lady and his gun in the dirt fifteen feet away, they had totally forgotten that fact.

"Oh, shit!" yelled Nate.

The grins had now turned to sheer panic as both men fumbled to reload.

J.T. brought his right hand up off the ground and rolled onto his right shoulder as he pulled the short-barrel Colt from the shoulder rig hanging under his left arm and snapped off two quick shots. Charlie let out a yell as one of the bullets hit the gun in his hand and sent it flying into the kitchen. The second shot hit a post on the porch, sending splinters of wood into Nate's left cheek. He let out a howl. Grabbing Charlie, Nate retreated back through the kitchen door and out of sight.

Before J.T. could fire again, three shots kicked up the dirt around him. Tom Baxter was firing down at him from a second-story window. J.T. scrambled for the porch on his hands and knees as two more bullets slammed into the ground only inches from his legs. Taking a minute to catch his breath, J.T. listened for any sounds coming from the house. But there was only silence. Shucking the two spent cartridges from his gun, he replaced them.

Another minute went by, and there came a low moan from behind him. J.T. looked back to his right. The madam was starting to come around. Just beyond her he saw his Peacemaker on the ground, illuminated by the glow from the lamp in the kitchen. Keeping his gun trained on the upstairs window, he eased himself out away from the porch. When he was within a few feet of the Peacemaker, he leaped forward, snatched it off the ground, and rolled out of the light. He had expected a hail of bullets to come raining down, but there was nothing.

On his feet now, and with a gun in each hand, J.T. jumped on the porch and dashed into the kitchen. It was empty. Moving to the hallway, he kept one gun pointed up toward the staircase and the other straight down the hallway. There was no telling where the Baxters were or from which direction they might come at him. Every muscle in his body was coiled tight as a wagon spring. This was a game he'd played many times, and it never got any easier. It not only took steel nerve and catlike reflexes, but a willingness to come face-to-face with the dark horseman of death. He could be waiting at the top of the stairs, or lurking in a dark corner of any of these rooms. It was not a game for the faint of heart or those who were not willing to die.

All of J.T.'s senses were alert. He darted his eyes from the stairs to the dark recesses of each room he passed, expecting at any second to see a flash from the darkness and feel hot lead rip its way through his body, but he continued on, making his way to the lobby. Where the hell were they? He had expected a gunfight long before now. Moving to the room where this had all started, he glanced down to the floor and the bloody body of Morgan Baxter. If only the old man had stayed in that room a few minutes longer, this thing would be over now.

The sudden sound of gunshots and a woman's scream sent J.T. running out onto the front porch. There were more shots and more screaming. It was coming from somewhere behind the blacksmith shop. He heard horses, then caught a glimpse of three figures riding hell-bent for leather past the general store and off into the darkness of the night.

"Dammit all to hell!" he said as he broke from the porch and ran toward the blacksmith shop. Rounding the corner, he stopped and stared down at the Baxter brothers' final act of carnage. The blacksmith, two of the cowboys, and another one of the girls lay dead. The madam cradled the dead girl's head in her lap, quietly rocking her back and forth. The other girls were gathered around her and crying. A few feet away, the cowboy called Willy was kneeling over the bodies of his two friends. Looking up at J.T. with tears in his eyes, he asked, "Why? Nobody here even had a gun. Why'd they have to do this?"

J.T. shook his head. He had no answers for the young cowboy. Near the corner of the shop, the girl who had been sitting with the big man earlier now sat beside his lifeless body, holding his hand in her own. J.T. suddenly remembered Coe Baxter.

Hurrying around the building to the corral, he was surprised and relieved to find the boy was still hog-tied to the corner post. In all the confusion and excitement to get their horses and get out of there, the brothers hadn't noticed their youngest brother in the darkness at the far end of the corral. With the gag firmly in place, Coe Baxter's moaning and mumbling could not be heard over the stomping and commotion of the horses.

J.T. walked up to the boy, cocking the .45 and staring hard at him for a moment. It was all he could do to stop himself from shooting the kid right there simply because he was a Baxter. But the anger soon subsided and he put the gun away. Stepping up to the corral fence, he hooked his arms over the top rail and silently tallied up the cost of his actions this night. On the plus side, he had killed one Baxter and had another in irons. At least that was something. But at what cost? On the bad side of the ledger, the one dead Baxter wasn't even wanted for anything. Three had gotten away, and worst of all, three men and two woman were dead. Innocent victims of the whole damn thing.

J.T. tried to figure how he could have done things different. But it really didn't matter anymore. What was done was done. He had learned a long time ago that you can never go back. He could stand there all night and pick apart everything he'd done and it wouldn't make any difference. The best thing to do was to let it go and move on. A man in his profession could do nothing else.

Removing the gag from the boy's mouth, J.T. began untying the rope from the post. Coe Baxter grinned as he said, "Didn't get 'em, did you, bounty man? Well, they'll be back. You hear me? They'll be back for me, an' then there's gonna be hell to pay. You just wait an' see."

J.T. stopped what he was doing and stepped back. Staring into the boy's eyes with a look as cold and hard as any Coe Baxter had ever seen, J.T. suddenly backhanded him across the mouth. The blow snapped the kid's head back, and blood began to flow from a busted lip, down Coe's chin, and onto his shirt. Every vein in J.T.'s neck was throbbing as he once again fought the urge to take all his anger and frustration out on the helpless boy. He pointed a finger in the kid's face.

"Don't say another damn word. You hear me? One more word—just one. An' I swear to God I'll put you in a grave next to that damn old man of yours, right here and now."

J.T.'s actions had startled Coe, but the pain of the blow had been immediately forgotten at the mention of his father.

"Is my pa dead?" he asked.

"Damn right he is. An' you're gonna be next if you don't keep your mouth shut. I'm mad, kid. Killin' mad! A lot of innocent people died tonight because of your brothers. Just don't say anything more. I mean it!"

Coe could tell by the look in the man's eyes that he meant exactly what he said. He wisely decided the best thing for him to do for now was just what the man said. Keep his mouth shut. As J.T. continued to untie him, young Coe tried to feel some type of remorse for his father, but like the others, there was nothing there. Morgan Baxter had beaten it out of him long ago.

Daylight was just breaking as J.T. placed Coe's hands behind his back and locked the irons in place. The kid had followed the man's advice and hadn't said another word.

Placing the kid up on his horse, J.T. walked over and mounted Toby. Taking the reins of Coe's horse, he led him out of the corral. The two rode out of Boone's Ferry, leaving the surviving residents to mourn their losses and bury the dead.

NINE

J.T. HAD PICKED up the trail of the brothers a few miles from Boone's Ferry. They were headed southeast. Normally he would have begun a dogged pursuit, riding hard and fast to close the distance between him and his prey. But that was not going to be possible with young Coe Baxter in tow. He had considered taking him back to Nacogdoches to be held in the jail there, but that would cost him two days. Besides that, there was the fact that the Baxters had friends in that town and it was a good bet they would try to break the kid out first chance they got. J.T. couldn't see Sheriff Bowlin putting up much of a fight if that were to happen. No, the only way was for him to stay on their trail and keep the kid with him. It would slow him down, but it was better than losing the two days and possibly the kid as well.

Coe hadn't said a word since they'd left Boone's Ferry. Now, as the sun began to set, they prepared to make camp for the night. J.T. helped him down from his horse and removed the irons.

"I'm givin' you five minutes of privacy to take care of your business over there in those bushes. You give me any trouble, any trouble at all, kid, an' I swear, I won't think twice about puttin' a bullet in your head an' leavin' you for the wolves. You understand?"

Coe Baxter rubbed at his sore, chaffed wrists and nodded as he replied, "Yeah. I reckon you made it clear enough."

J.T. nodded. "Good. Now get to it. We got work to do puttin' this camp together."

Under the watchful eye of his captor, Coe moved off into the bushes. A short time later he returned. He went straight to his horse, removed the saddle and outfit, then tied him off next to Toby. Seeing J.T. remove a frying pan, coffeepot, and other gear from his pack, Coe began to gather wood for a fire, making sure he was always within sight of the bounty man. Carrying the first load to the center of the camp, he piled it next to a fire pit J.T. had fashioned from rocks, then went out again to gather more wood.

Coe's arms were nearly full with the second load as he bent down to pick up a few more pieces. As he did, he paused and looked back toward the camp. J.T. had the fire going and was busy cutting up potatoes over the frying pan. His back was to him. Lying there on the ground was a solid piece of wood nearly two feet long. It would make the perfect club. Kneeling down, Coe placed it on the bottom of the pile.

His plan was simple. He would carry the wood back to the same spot he had the first time. Keeping one hand wrapped firmly around the club hidden on the bottom, he would bend over, dump the other wood, and at the same time swing the club in a backward motion, catching the bounty hunter square in the face. He'd then grab his gun and kill him if he had to. It was a daring plan that could easily get him killed, but Coe felt he had little choice. Once they had him locked up, there would be the trial, a guilty verdict, and a quick hanging for sure.

J.T. still had his back to him as the boy approached. His stomach was a jumble of nerves and sweat had broken out on his forehead. He was scared to death. But the thought of hanging drove him on.

J.T. hadn't looked back in the kid's direction once. Now, as he busied himself making coffee, the boy took a couple of steps past him and was about to bend over to drop the wood. In a low, matter-of-fact tone, J.T. said, "You done made one mistake in your life, kid, an' you're about to make another one."

Coe's heart skipped a couple of beats. Remaining half bent over, he looked back at J.T. The shoulder holster was empty. The .45 lay on a rock next to the bounty man's right boot.

"Now, son. If you figure that stick's a match for a Colt .45, you go right ahead an' give it a try."

Coe Baxter was caught totally by surprise. How did the bounty man know what he was going to do? The man hadn't turned his way once since he'd found that club. Dumping the wood, club and all, the kid sat down on the ground across from the bounty man.

"How'd you know I was up to somethin'?" he asked.

J.T. didn't look up as he pushed the taters around in the pan with a fork. "That's easy, kid. If I was in your place, I'd have been looking for the biggest damn club I could find and hope I had a plan that would work."

Coe let out a sigh and leaned back against a fallen tree. "Yeah, but there's one big difference. You'd have had the guts to follow it through. So would my brothers.

Guess that makes me the only damn coward in the bunch."

J.T. pushed the taters to the side and tossed in some bacon. As it crackled and sizzled, he looked over at the boy. "No, son, that don't make you no coward. Just makes you smarter than most, that's all."

As night came and they finished eating, J.T. relaxed and rolled himself a cigarette. He had lost his only two remaining cigars during the fight back at Boone's Ferry. He'd already cussed himself for not having bought more of them while he was in Austin. Coe Baxter hadn't said much since J.T.'s remark about being smart. The comment had caught the boy off guard. Coming from a man as hard as J.T. Law seemed to be, that was a compliment. His own pa had never called him smart; sonofabitch, dumb bastard, and idiot, but never smart.

J.T. lit his smoke and offered the bag of tobacco to the boy, who turned it down.

"How old are you, kid?" asked J.T.

"Seventeen. Why?"

"Oh, I don't know. Somehow you just don't seem to fit this kind of business. How'd you get yourself mixed up in it anyway?"

"To be honest with you, I don't rightly know. I guess I was more scared of what my pa would do if I didn't go along than what the law would do to me if I did. He was a mean, hard man, our pa. Always drinkin' an' beatin' up on Ma an' us kids. He got worse after she died of the fever. Guess I oughta feel bad he's dead, but I don't. I don't feel nothin'. Hell, if you hadn't killed him, I really think Nate would have, sooner or later."

J.T. watched the boy as he talked. He began to realize that young Coe Baxter wasn't the cold, hard killer his brothers were. He was just a boy who had gotten caught up in a situation not of his making. But there was one thing J.T. had to know.

"Back in Nacogdoches. You have a part in the killin' of that girl and those two Rangers?"

Coe lowered his head and stared for a long time at the fire before he answered.

"I was there, but I never fired a shot. An' that's the God's honest truth. I . . . I knew that girl. Her name was Ruby. She wasn't much older than me. I told Nate the whole thing was a bad idea, but all that got me was the back of his hand."

"What about when they circled 'em an shot 'em to pieces?"

"I saw 'em all go down when they fired, but when they went for the Rangers, I went to try and help Ruby. But there was nothin' anybody could do for her—God, those shotguns made such a mess . . . it . . . it . . ."

J.T. thought the kid was going to be sick any second. His face had gone pale and he clutched his stomach. It was understandable. A ten-gauge shotgun would have opened up that girl like a gutted buffalo. J.T. knew from experience. It was a sight that remained with you forever. Regaining his composure, Coe continued.

"I was standing next to her body when the next thing I know, there was all this shootin' goin' on behind me. Tom even reloaded and kept firin' after Nate and Charlie walked away. It was like he just went crazy. I should've rode out right then. But where would I go? I was already wanted, and crazy or not, they were still my brothers."

J.T. tossed some wood on the fire. "You ever killed anybody since this thing started, Coe?"

"I don't rightly know. I mean, I done a lot of shootin' during the bank robberies, but most of the time I just shot up in the air or at a window once in a while. Nate said we needed to scare the people outta the street. Make 'em too scared to mess with us, you know. Hell, I ain't no good with a damn popper. Nate's the shootist in the family. Him an' Charlie both. Me . . . I'm better with a rifle."

"So Nate's the gunhand, is he?"

"Yes, sir. Quick as a snake and hardly ever misses what he's shootin' at. Charlie, he's slower on the pull, but got a damn good eye."

It was getting late and J.T. was tired. Reaching into his saddlebag, he brought out a pair of irons with a chain attached.

"You won't be needin' those, Mr. Law. I figure you got me fair and square. I don't plan on runnin' anymore. Don't reckon I'd get far anyway."

Crossing over to where the kid sat, J.T. dropped the irons down next to him. "I'm sure you mean what you say, son. But I'll sleep a lot better knowin' you're fixed to that tree behind you. So let's get 'em on."

Coe started to argue the point, but knew it would do no good. Silently, he snapped the irons on and watched the chain being wrapped around the tree, then padlocked. Accepting his fate, the boy stretched out, pulled his blanket up on himself, then rested his head back on his saddle.

J.T. repositioned his saddle and lay down on his bedroll. Removing both his guns, he placed one on each side of the blanket within easy reach. By the time he had pulled his blanket up, he glanced over and saw the kid was already asleep. Resting his head on the saddle, J.T. stared up at the stars that filled the Texas sky. He was thinking about his conversation with the seventeen-year-old boy who now lay asleep across from him. A boy whose own father and brothers had brought him to this point in his young life. A life that had known nothing but abuse and violence.

J.T. know about violence. He was eighteen. When the War Between the States began he had joined the Texas

Confederate Calvary and headed north to fight. By age twenty, he had fought in no less than nine battles, been wounded twice, and gone from being a private to the rank of captain. They said he was a natural-born leader.

When a close friend had been captured by the Yankees, they had built a bonfire and hanging the man upside down, had lowered him, screaming and begging, into the flames. It was J.T. who had found what was left of him. He had buried him, then set out after the men who had done this terrible deed. Tracking them over one hundred miles, he'd finally caught up to them and killed them all, including the Yankee captain who had been in charge. The man had fallen to his knees begging for young J.T. to spare his life, but J.T. had shot him six times, then pulled another pistol and shot him six more. Much in the same fashion as Tom Baxter had done to the Rangers.

By the time he was twenty-one, he found himself riding side by side with Cole Younger and Frank James. He soon discovered that fighting in a guerrilla war moved the violence and killing to a whole new level. It was total war. Ruthless and bloody, with no quarter expected nor given. At times, a young J.T. found himself growing sick of the constant fighting and killing and wanting to leave. To go back to Texas. So why didn't he just ride away? He didn't know why. But he never did. He stayed until it was over.

And now, here he was, in this time and place, with a young boy who'd had his chance to ride away when that chance came, but hadn't. The only difference between them was that Coe Baxter would hang for it.

TEN

KNEELING DOWN FOR a closer look at the tracks he had been following for the last four days, J.T. studied them for a moment, then stood and stared off to the west. Nate Baxter and his two brothers had been moving south-southwest ever since hightailing it out of Boone's Ferry. Now they had suddenly changed direction and were heading due west. Judging from the tracks he had just found, the reason for that change was clear. One of the boys was riding a horse with a bad left front leg. The depth of the imprint was an indication that the horse wasn't going to go much farther. They'd have to find a replacement, and find one soon.

It was a good sign for J.T. The animal had already caused them to slow their pace, and even with Coe in tow, J.T. was slowly, but surely, closing the distance between them. The way he had it figured, he was no more than ten to twelve hours behind them. If not for the kid, he would have already caught up to this bunch. But he wasn't going to say anything about that right now. Coe Baxter was already feeling bad enough as it was. He had been so sure that Nate and the others would come back for him. But with the passing of each new day and the further south they rode, it became quite clear to the young cowboy that his brothers had no such intention. They had left him to fend for himself. In effect, he felt, they had written him off.

Climbing back in the saddle, J.T. brought out a canteen, took a drink, then passed it over to Coe.

"They still heading south?" asked the boy before he lifted the canteen.

"No. Tracks are leading due west. One of your brothers has a horse that's going lame."

Coe passed the canteen back. "Why west?"

"There ain't nothin' or nobody for fifty miles south, but there's a few small ranches and settlements maybe fifteen—twenty miles west of here. Only place they can get fresh horses."

Coe looked off to the west, then back at the bounty man.

"Mr. Law. I been thinking 'bout what you said the first night out. You know, about whether or not I'd killed anybody. Well, since I haven't, you think maybe there's a chance a jury could see their way clear to send me off to prison, 'stead of to the hangman?"

Funny the kid would ask that question. J.T. had been wondering the same thing the last few days. True to his word, Coe hadn't given him any trouble since that first night. In camp, he took care of the horses, gathered the firewood, made the coffee, and cleaned the cook gear. At night, the two had talked about his mother, horses, and even a girl back in Steeles Grove who had stolen his heart when he was fourteen.

When J.T. had set out after the Baxters, Coe Baxter

had been no more than a name on a warrant, but now, for the first time in all his years as a bounty hunter, he found himself concerned about what was going to happen to a man he'd gone after. He'd taken a liking to the kid and having spent the last few days with him, was convinced that growing up under different circumstances, Coe Baxter could just as easily been another Billy Tyler.

"I don't rightly know, boy. I suppose if you had a lawyer that was a good talker, it might be possible. I just happen to know a couple of fellows in Fort Worth, silver-tongued devils both of 'em. We get back, I'll see if maybe I can't get 'em to look into your case. Fair enough?"

For the first time since J.T. had hog-tied him to a corral post, he saw a flicker of hope come alive in the boy's eyes and a smile cross his face.

"Now, I ain't promisin' nothing, kid. You understand that, don't you?"

"Yes, sir, I understand. An' I thank you."

As they turned their horses west, Coe Baxter's spirits had been lifted. How ironic it was, he thought, that the only person who seemed to care about what happened to him now was the man who had been sent out to arrest him or kill him. Of course, as Mr. Law had said, there were no guarantees. But at least for the moment anyway, there was hope.

The faint sound of gunfire coming from the hills to the north caused J.T. to rein in. He listened again. It was still a long way off, but it was definitely gunfire.

"What is it? What's wrong?" asked Coe, who hadn't picked up on the sound yet.

"Gunfire! An' a hell of a lot of it. Maybe two, three miles north. Other side of those hills there."

Coe rose slightly in his stirrups. He still couldn't hear anything. But if this man said it was there, then it was there.

"Think it could be my brothers?"

"Don't know. But we're sure as hell gonna find out. You keep up with me now, you hear?"

"Yes, sir. I'll try."

Putting the spurs to their horses, they rode at a full gallop, Coe matching J.T. stride for stride. As they closed in on the base of the hills, Coe could hear the gunfire clearly now. J.T. was right. There was a lot of it. It sounded like a full-scale battle was in progress.

Coming off the plains at full stride, both horses moved quickly up the slope of the first hill. J.T. pulled up just short of the crest. Swinging down out of the saddle, he pulled his Winchester from the saddle boot and his field glasses from his saddlebags. Staying low, he made his way up to the top of the hill. Coe was following close behind. Lying on their stomachs, the two surveyed the scene below.

"Jesus," said Coe. "Comanches! An' they got somebody in a bad fix down there."

J.T. brought up his glasses and scanned the terrain. The hillsides were swarming with the Comanches Abe Covington and half of Texas were searching for. And apparently, someone had had the misfortune to find them. Moving the glasses down to the floor of the canyon below, J.T. uttered, "I'll be damned."

"What is it? Is it my brothers?" asked Coe with nervous excitement in his voice.

"No. It's a detachment of Rangers out of Austin."

Coe strained his young eyes, then asked, "How can you tell that from up here?"

J.T. still had his glasses focused on the small group, which had been forced into a cluster of boulders back against the canyon wall.

"Cause the fellow I'm looking at right now ain't much older than you. Name's Billy Tyler, Texas Ranger in Captain Abe Covington's command out of Austin. An' you're right. Them boys got theirself in a tight fix down there."

Moving the glasses around the tight-knit circle of Rangers, J.T. could see that they were in a bad way. Four men lay sprawled on the ground outside the circle. They weren't moving. He figured they were dead, but the Indians still threw a shot or two at them, apparent by the small puffs of dust he saw rise around the bodies every so often. The Indians were making sure they were dead. Back among the rocks, he saw three wounded Rangers propped up against the wall to the rear. Their shirts were covered in blood. Counting Billy Tyler, there were only seven Rangers still standing and able to fight.

"How many Comanches you figure?" asked Coe.

J.T. had made a hurried count. "Thirty-five to forty."

Another fifteen lay scattered motionless on the ground and in the rocks around the Rangers. Billy and his fellow Rangers had made the Comanches pay a price for backing them into a corner. But it was only a matter of time before they were overrun by the sheer force of numbers. They needed help and they needed it now.

"Come on," said J.T. as he backed down from the crest.

Going into his saddlebags again, J.T. brought out the irons with the chain attached.

"Sorry, kid. But I'm not gonna have time to be watchin' you. Come on over here an' let me switch these irons."

Coe Baxter wasn't moving.

"Now come on, kid. I ain't got time for this. Them boys down there need my help an' we're runnin' out of time."

Coe shook his head. "No, sir. There's no way I'm puttin' them irons on. Might as well me shoot me now. Supposin' you and them boys down there get yourselves killed. Where's that leave me? I'll tell you where. Sittin' here trussed up like a damn turkey ready for the spit. An' you know I'm right. I'd rather you just shoot me here and now than be left to them Comanche down there."

J.T. had to admit the boy had a good point. "Then just what the hell am I supposed to do with you?"

Coe didn't hesitate answering. "You take these damn irons off and give me that rifle. That's what. These boys need all the help they can get. Like I told you, I ain't much with a handgun, but ain't many can match me with a long gun."

Damn, this kid had more brass than J.T. had given him credit for.

"An I suppose you're just gonna hand over that rifle when this is all over. That right?"

"Yes, sir. Told you I wasn't runnin' anymore an' I meant it. Figure your idea about the lawyers is about my only way outta this fix I got myself into. I done made one mistake, Mr. Law. I don't intend to make another. I'll have to ask you to trust me, I reckon."

J.T. thought on it for a moment. He'd done a lot of crazy things in his lifetime, but this one just could be his last. The volume of gunfire picked up from down in the canyon. That could only mean the Indians were preparing to make their big charge.

"Oh, what the hell. Those damn Comanche will more'n likely kill us all anyway."

Dropping the chain irons to the ground, J.T. took out his key and unlocked the ones the kid was wearing. Pulling a spare box of bullets from his saddlebags, he tossed them to Coe.

"Guess we'll just find out how good you are with that long gun. You move around that small crest and get yourself a good position on the right. I'm gonna move down the hill on the left side. I'll have to get in closer to 'em to do any good with these .45's. Make every shot count, kid."

Coe nodded that he understood, and took off for the right side to find a position. J.T. moved to the left and down, working his way through the rocks, all the while wondering if he had just signed his own death warrant. What was to stop Coe Baxter from blowing his head off and riding away? He was, after all, taking this boy back for trial. A trial that could very easily put a rope around his neck. But it was too late to worry about it now. What was done was done. He could only hope that he hadn't misjudged the character of the young cowboy.

A few seconds later, Coe put J.T.'s mind at ease. A Comanche, hiding in the rocks above the bounty man, rose with a tomahawk in his hand, and would have caved in J.T.'s skull if it hadn't been for a rifle shot from above that hit the Comanche in the forehead.

Wiping blood and brains from his coat, J.T. looked back up the hill. Coe waved to him, then shifted his rifle fire to another target across the way. The kid had just saved J.T. Law's life and put to rest any question of his ability with a rifle.

With a Colt in each hand. J.T. dodged in and out of the rocks, working his way downward, surprising and killing a total of five Comanches along the way who had no idea anyone was behind them. The kid's rifle was taking a toll as well. Counting the forehead shot, J.T. saw six go down that he attributed to Coe. And Coe was still going strong. Pausing only long enough to reload.

From inside the circle of Rangers, Billy Tyler watched in momentary confusion as more and more of the Comanches were being hit and dropping like flies. He knew he and his fellow Rangers weren't hitting that many of 'em. That firing was coming from somewhere else. Across the valley floor he saw someone moving among the rocks and it wasn't a Comanche. It was a white man. He had practically cleared the left hill of Comanche all by himself. Looking up along the ridge, Billy spotted someone with a rifle. The long gun was thinning the ranks of the Indians with nearly every shot.

"Hey, you fellas! We got help out there from somebody."

Billy pointed out the positions to the others as one asked, "Any idea who it is?"

"Don't know. But with shootin' like that, I'm damn glad they're on our side."

As more and more of their number went down, the Comanches finally figured out that they were caught in a cross fire. Somehow someone had gotten behind them and their losses were mounting fast. From the rocks, a Comanche yelled out a command and the Indians began a full-scale retreat to the far side of the canyon, more concerned with getting away now than with killing the few remaining Rangers.

Five minutes or so passed without a shot being fired. The Comanches had had enough and pulled out, taking their wounded with them. Feeling it was safe, Rangers Billy Tyler and Tom Overhalt walked out from the cover of the rocks and into the open. Shading their eyes with their hands, they were trying to spot whoever it was who had broken the backs of the Indians with such devastating accuracy, but they couldn't see anyone on the ridge or in the rocks.

"I wonder who that was up there," said Overhalt.

Billy was about to say the same thing when he saw two riders coming their way. He recognized the big buckskin at once.

"Hell, we should'd know'd. Looky here who's comin'."

Overhalt turned to see J.T. and a young cowboy coming down the canyon. Guerrilla or not, Overhalt and the other Rangers were glad to see the bounty man.

Billy Tyler laid his rifle back on his shoulder and smiled up at J.T. as he approached. "Damn glad to see ya', John Thomas."

Overhalt walked over to J.T. and reaching up, extended his hand to the man.

"You sure as shootin' pulled our fat out of the fire today, J.T. We owe you."

J.T. took the man's hand and shook it firmly. "You boys would've done the same for me."

While the wounded were being tended to, J.T., Overhalt, and Tyler all stood off to the side talking.

"Who's the kid?" asked Billy.

"That's the fella with the rifle that was firing from the ridge up there. Boy's damn good with a Winchester."

"Ya ain't gotta' tell me. He was droppin' them Indians like it was a Sunday turkey shoot. What's his name?"

J.T. showed a slight grin. "Coe Baxter."

Overhalt and Tyler looked at each other, then to the kid, and back to J.T.

"That's a joke, right?" said Overhalt.

"It's no joke, Ranger. That there is Coe Baxter, all right."

"Well I'll be damned," said Tyler. "That one of the Baxter brothers? The same ones that killed our boys up in Nacogdoches? I thought you had warrants for them."

"Do. That's one of 'em. The youngest."

"Well, if he's your prisoner, you wanta tell us why the hell you'd give him a loaded rifle? You took a hell of a chance, didn't you, J.T.?"

"Not really. You boys needed help, an' you needed it fast. He offered his help an' gave me his word."

"His word," exclaimed Billy, who took off his hat and scratched his head, saying, "Okay, John Thomas. Ya wanta tell us what's goin' on here?"

J.T. smiled. "Yeah, I suppose I'd better. Have a seat on this here rock boys an' I'll tell you a story."

The bounty man told them of his trip to Nacogdoches and then Steeles Grove. About his capture of Coe and the fight at Boone's Ferry. He concluded by telling them of his conversations with the boy and why he'd felt he could trust him. By the time he'd finished, both Rangers were looking at Coe Baxter in a different light.

"Damnedest story I ever heard," said Overhalt. "So what're you gonna do with him now?"

"I was wantin' to send him back with you boys. I know there's hard feelin's toward the Baxters because of what happen to Longley and Crowder. But I'm countin' on you boys to make sure the other Rangers know this boy had no part in it. Will you do that?"

Overhalt slapped J.T. on the back. "Said we owe you. If that's what you want, you got it. Me an' Billy'll set the other boys straight about the kid. Don't you worry none."

Billy nodded in agreement. "You can count on it, J.T. Hell, wasn't for that kid an' his eye with that long gun, we might all be missin' our hair."

"That's a fact, Billy. An I'd like you to make sure folks know that. It just might help him at his trial."

With the wounded loaded up and the dead buried, the remnants of what was left of the Ranger unit were ready to start on the long journey back to headquarters. J.T. had taken young Coe aside and explained to him what was going to happen. He reminded him to keep his spirits up and not to give the Rangers any trouble. He had earned their respect by his actions and J.T. wanted to keep it that way.

As J.T. mounted to leave, Coe Baxter reached up and shook his hand.

"I wanta thank you, John Thomas. You gave me somethin' I never had before."

"What's that, son?"

"Respect."

ELEVEN

FREE OF COE Baxter, J.T. picked up the trail once again. Now he began the pursuit in earnest. Four hours of hard riding brought him to a small ranch outside the town of Dailyville. The sight of three badly worn horses in the corral told him he was too late. The brothers had already changed horses and were on the run again.

Riding up to the front porch, J.T. hoped to find someone who could tell him how long the men had been gone. But when he went up to the door to knock, it opened by itself. He called out, but no one answered. Stepping inside, he saw why. A man, a woman, and two small children lay dead in the floor. There was blood everywhere. Pulling his gun, J.T. went through the house searching each room. He doubted he would find anyone, but it didn't hurt to be ready. Outside, in back of the house, he found the bodies of two cowboys. They had been killed in the doorway of the bunkhouse. The Baxters had added another six victims to their reign of terror across Texas.

Going back into the house, the hardened bounty man looked down at the pitiful faces of the two small children. Neither could have been more than seven or eight. Pulling a lace-edged cloth from the table behind him, he knelt down and folded their small hands onto their chests, then covered them with the tablecloth. He had gone after countless men in his lifetime as a bounty hunter, some as ruthless and hard as any on the frontier, but in all that time he had never seen such senseless killing, simply for the pure pleasure of it. These weren't men, they were rabid dogs.

Finding a shovel in the barn, J.T. set about digging graves for the six people whose misfortune it had been to encounter the Baxter brothers. The holes dug, he carefully placed each in a grave, being especially mindful of the two children. With each shovelful of dirt he placed over them, he thought of a different way to kill each of the men who had done this. Returning to the barn, he found a hammer, nails, and wood and fashioned six crosses. Driving them into the ground at the head of each grave, he tossed the shovel aside.

Returning to the house, he found pencil and paper and wrote a detailed account of what he had seen upon his arrival at the home and his actions afterward. If any additional information were needed about the men who had committed this crime, the authorities were to contact Captain Abe Covington of the Texas Rangers in Austin. Signing the letter, J.T. stood and took a final look around the room. He had done all he could.

Walking out of the house, he made a silent vow to the two dead children he was leaving behind. He wasn't going to try to capture these men. He was going to kill them. Kill all three of them. There would be no mercy, no quarter given. He promised that as he rode away. And John Thomas Law had never broke a promise in his life.

Two more days and nights of hard riding brought him to the small town of San Patricio. Through inquires in the Spanish sector he discovered that Nate Baxter and his brothers had passed through the town less than five hours earlier. They had crossed the Nueces River and were believed to be headed for Corpus Christi.

Easing Toby into the waters of the Nueces, J.T. could feel his blood beginning to stir. He was quickly closing the distance on the Baxters. Soon, very soon, they were going to face the wrath of retribution for their crimes. As tired as he and Toby both were, he kept pushing himself on. By late evening the tracks told him he was less than an hour behind them. Now, if only they'd camp for the night, he'd have them right where he wanted them.

NATE BAXTER POURED himself a cup of coffee and sat back on a log, staring out at the darkness of the night. Tom lay across from the fire, wrapped in his blankets, asleep. Charlie was just coming back in from checking the horses. Pouring himself some coffee, he joined Nate on the log.

"Ya think he's still comin'?" Charlie asked.

"Hell, yes. He's out there somewhere. I can feel it. He ain't gonna' give up. Ain't his style."

Charlie took a sip of his coffee, then said, "I figure he's a day, or maybe two, behind us. Depends on whether or not he had Coe with him when he left Boone's Ferry. If he did, that'd slow him down considerable, wouldn't ya think?"

Nate spat, then answered, "Hell. Wouldn't slow me down none. I'd just shoot the damn kid and keep comin'."

A look of concern came over Charlie. "Ya think he done killed Coe?"

"Hell, how should I know, Charlie. Don't really matter much now, does it?"

Charlie was about to say something else when suddenly both men heard the sound of approaching horses. Tossing their coffee cups aside, they grabbed their rifles. Charlie kicked Tom in the butt to wake him, then told him to grab his rifle and join them in the woods. There were riders coming. Moving back out of the light of the campfire, the brothers levered a round into each of their Winchesters and waited in the darkness for the unexpected visitors.

There were eight of them. All Mexicans. The heavyset man in front, with the thick mustache, a wicked scar on his cheek, and a pockmarked face, appeared to be the leader. They had ridden straight into the camp, and now sat their horses waiting for someone to appear.

"Hola!" shouted the leader. "Where is everyone? Amigos, come out. We mean you no harm. We are friends. Come out."

Charlie stared long and hard at the man out front, then whispered to his brother. "Nate. Ya know who that fellow is, don't ya?"

"Yep. Juan Valdez. The bandit. Been raidin' Texas for years."

"That's right. What'd ya figure he's doin' here?"

"Hell, let's go ask him."

Charlie started to protest, but it was to late. Nate had already walked out of the shadows into the light of the campfire.

"Ah," said the bandit. "There you are. Why do you hide from us, Señor Baxter? We too are bandits, or as you gringos say, outlaws."

Keeping the butt of his rifle pressed against his thigh and pointed in the general direction of the riders, Nate asked, "What d'ya want here, Valdez?"

The old bandit smiled broadly, then turned to his men and laughed.

"You see, compadraes? Even this gringo knows the great bandit Juan Valdez."

Charlie stepped out of the darkness now. His rifle was at the ready.

"My brother ask ya a question, mister."

Valdez's expression never changed. If anything, the smile got wider.

"Ah. The second Baxter. But there are three of you riding together, no? Where is the third?"

Tom had moved around behind the group, and now stepped out of the dark behind the riders.

"Right, here, friend."

"Damn! I like this. You are cautious men. That is good."

"Cut the shit, Valdez. What d'ya want here?" ask Nate.

"Ah, you gringos an' your expressions. I have come here to make you a proposition, Señor Nate. It could prove very profitable for us both if you will hear me out. May I get down?"

Valdez swung his big body down out of the saddle and began rubbing his ass. "Ah, thank you, Señor. I am not sure if my horse is getting harder or my ass softer. Here, come now. Put the guns away, my friend. You have no need of them. Let us have some whiskey and talk business like gentlemen. What you say, Señor Nate? Amigos, okay?"

Nate Baxter didn't trust this crafty old bastard as far as he could throw him, and he doubted seriously if they would be interested in any deal this cutthroat had to offer. Still, it would be nice to have him and his men around if that damn bounty hunter showed up. That would make the odds eleven to one. Even J.T. Law wasn't that damn good.

Raising his rifle barrel up in the air, then dropping it back on his shoulder, he said, "Why not? You say somethin' about whiskey?"

J.T. SILENTLY EASED himself back from the camp site on his stomach until he was sure he was far enough away not to be seen or heard. The unexpected arrival of Juan Valdez and his men certainly had complicated things. J.T. had only been seconds away from jumping up and blowing the hell out of all three of the Baxter boys when the old Mexican bandit appeared. Over the years, J.T. and Valdez's trails had crossed a number of times. The old bandit was practically a legend in parts of Texas and Mexico. Their last encounter had come early last summer, down near Brownsville. J.T. had had a warrant for the arrest of a bank robber and killer named Ben Kingsley. Kingsley had traveled with a band of outlaw *vaqueros*, and one of them had just happened to be the nephew of Juan Valdez. When Kingsley resisted arrest, J.T. had killed him, along with the nephew and three other *vaqueros*. When Valdez got the news, they said he went a little crazy, vowing to hunt down J.T. and nail him to a tree.

The old bastard had almost pulled it off too. Outside of Waco, they had ambushed J.T. in an arroyo. In the running gun battle that followed, J.T. had suffered two minor wounds. Juan Valdez, on the other hand, had lost three men and almost been killed himself. J.T. had shot the bandit's horse during the chase. The horse's front legs had folded and Valdez had gone flying from the saddle, face-first into a cactus grove, ripping his left cheek open to the bone and ending up with over fifty cactus spines stuck all over his face. This was the first time J.T. had seen the old bandit since that little altercation.

Now, sitting atop Toby in the darkness and staring

across the open plain at the campfire flickering a hundred yards away, J.T. considered his next move. He could wait and hope that Valdez and his men left before morning. But what if they didn't? What if the two outfits joined forces for this proposition the old bandit had mentioned? How long would it be before J.T. could catch the Baxters alone then? A day? A week? A month? No, he wasn't going to wait that long. As the prairie breeze blew across his face, J.T. began to remember another time and place when he had sat a horse in the darkness and watched an enemy's campfire from a distance. Only he hadn't been alone that night.

IT WAS DURING the war and the place was Baxter Springs, Kansas. The campfire belong to a detachment of a hundred Yankees escorting a wagon train of supplies. Sitting to the left of J.T. that night had been his leader, Bloody Bill Anderson, and forty of the most deadly and feared guerrillas to ride the Kansas plains. To J.T.'s right had sat Cole Younger, and next to him, Frank and Jesse James. Although outnumbered almost two to one, Bloody Bill wasn't concerned. His boys had taken on odds far worse than that before. Some called him a genius, others called him a madman, but they all agreed on one thing. He was fearless and he loved to kill Yankees.

Every man that night carried four guns. Some as many as six. Two in saddle holsters attached to the saddlehorn, one on each hip, and two others in shoulder holsters, one under each arm. In guerrilla-style fighting there was no time for reloading. The object was to put out as much firepower as possible and to keep firing until your enemy was dead or sent packing. He could still hear the echoes of that frightening Rebel yell that rose from forty wild-eyed men as they stormed upon the unsuspecting Yankees like a Kansas twister coming out of the darkness. By the time it was over, eighty-six Yankees lay dead and the wagons of supplies were on their way to William Quantrill's headquarters. The element of surprise and firepower had again proved effective for Bloody Bill and the guerrillas of his command.

With the memory of that night and the faces of the dead children back at that ranch still fresh in his mind, J.T. now knew what he had to do. Stepping down from his horse, he said, "Hell, we're not waitin' anymore, Toby. Those damn child-killin' bastards are right out there, an' we're gonna take it to 'em tonight."

PULLING TWO NAVY Colts and his old saddle holster from his saddlebags, J.T. slipped the guns in place. Swinging back in the saddle, he could just imagine the smile that must be on Bloody Bill's face as he looked up from hell and saw one of his boys keeping up the old tradition.

J.T. started Toby at a walk, heading straight for the firelight in the distance. At thirty yards he went into a trot. At sixty yards, he picked up the pace, widening the gait. At eighty yards, J.T. drew both .45's and spurring Toby to a full gallop, let out a bloodcurdling Rebel yell that shattered the prairie silence.

"Gawdalmighty!" shouted Charlie. "What the hell is that?"

Nate and Valdez were on their feet and reaching for their guns, as were all the men in the camp. But they were too slow. J.T. came barreling out of the darkness, headlong into the center of the camp, both guns blazing, spitting death with every flash.

Two bandits on the outer edge of the camp were the first to go down. A third took a bullet in the back as he ran for the horses. Tom and Charlie Baxter tried to bring their rifles up, but were bowled over by the charging horse. Tom was sent sprawling into the campfire, while Charlie lay on the ground dazed by the blow. Nate dove behind a tree, but Valdez was too slow. He got off one shot before J.T. put two bullets in his gut, sending him to the ground.

In the terror and confusion of the moment, the bandits were firing wildly at the crazy gringo in the big buckskin, but weren't hitting anything. Charlie, his head clear now, jumped up from the ground, brought up the Winchester, and yelled, "I got you now, Goddamnit!"

But an instant before he fired, J.T. swung to the left side of the saddle. Charlie missed, but not J.T. Firing from under Toby's neck, he put a .45 bullet straight through the man's left eye.

Dropping the .45's, J.T. pulled out the Navy Colts and kept firing, killing another bandit who came at him with an ax. Nate rose to fire, but was driven back to the ground by two shots that took the bark off the tree only inches from his head.

"Jesus Christ!" yelled Nate. "He's a goddamn crazy man." He scrambled away from the tree on his hands and knees and circled in the darkness for the horses.

Tom Baxter narrowly rolled clear of Toby's hooves and crawled away. Seeing Nate break for the horses, he made a desperate dash for the woods. J.T. snapped off a shot in his direction and saw the man go down.

Valdez lay on the ground holding his stomach. He looked up just as Toby's front legs came down near the edge of the fire, sending a shower of red/orange cinders flying up in the air. They seemed to circle around the horse and rider. To Valdez it appeared as if the devil himself had risen up out of hell spewing death and destruction from the back of a demon horse.

Two bandits made a break for their horses. J.T. saw them and whirled Toby around. But before he could fire, another bandit ran forward, and planting his foot on the fallen tree near the fire, leaped into the air, knocking J.T. out of the saddle. Both men tumbled to the ground. The bandit regained his feet and in desperation, grabbed up a rifle by the barrel and swung it at J.T.'s head, barely missing him. J.T. kept crawling backward toward the fire as the man came at him again, swinging the rifle wildly back and forth. Feeling the heat from the fire on the back of his neck, J.T. rolled to his right, at the same time kicking out with his left boot and tripping the man, who fell forward into the flames. J.T. quickly rolled over on the man's back, shoved his face into the red-hot coals, then rolled off him. Seeing one of his Navy Colts on the ground, he grabbed it up and turned just as the screaming bandit rolled out of the fire. He was a horrible sight and his hair was on fire. J.T. mercifully put him out of his misery with a single shot to the head.

Climbing up on his knees, J.T. swung the pistol around in all directions, searching out another target, but there were none left. It was over. Rising to his feet, he could feel the energy begin to fade away. His hands began to shake slightly as he looked around the camp at the carnage he had caused.

Six men were dead, and old Valdez was close to it. Walking over to one of the bodies, he rolled it over. It was Charlie Baxter. His left eye was gone and there was a gaping hole in the back of his head. Moving to the tree line where he had seen Tom Baxter go down, he expected to find another body, but it wasn't there. J.T. had hit him. There was blood on the grass and the tree where the man had pulled himself up before running away. Walking back into the camp site, J.T. saw four horses were gone from the picket line, but all the saddles were still scattered on the ground. Nate and Tom Baxter, along with two of the bandits, had gotten away. Retrieving his weapons, he bent down to pick up one of the Navy Colts, and felt a sudden burning sensation along his left side. Raising his shirt, he was surprised to find an open gash where a bullet had barely missed its mark. With the excitement during the battle, he hadn't even felt the hit.

As he checked the wound more closely, he heard a laugh from behind him. He turned to find Valdez clutching his gun in both hands. It was all the old bandit could do to hold it up.

"My *pistola* pulls a little too much to the left. But I think maybe I have you now, John Thomas."

J.T. didn't move. He was holding a gun in each hand, but he had no way of knowing if either one still had a bullet left.

"I reckon you do, Juan," he said as he watched the bandit grimace from the pain of the two bullets in his stomach.

"Ah, you were magnificent, amigo. Your devil horse rearing up in the air amid the glowing cinders, his front legs kicking and your guns flashing. You had to see it to really appreciate the beauty of it. But trust me, my friend, it was truly *magnifico*."

"I'm glad you liked it."

Raising the gun a little higher, Valdez struggled to fight off the pain.

"I think I kill you now, John Thomas."

J.T. braced himself for the shot, but when the old man pulled the trigger, the ancient .44 he had carried for years misfired. Dropping his hands into his lap, Valdez shook his head. He was too weak to make another effort.

"Oh, amigo. You truly live a charmed life. I think maybe the Holy Mother watch over you."

Leaping forward, J.T. snatched the gun from the dying

man's hands. Opening it, he saw where the firing pin had dented the cartridge but it hadn't fired.

"You see, my friend," said Valdez, "I have killed many men with that gun. Never has it done this. I . . . Ooooh! Sweet mother . . . the pain . . . it is so bad."

J.T. reached forward, pushing the man's hands apart, and opened Valdez's shirt. The man's intestines were coming out. There was nothing J.T. could do. The old bandit moaned again and tried to draw his legs up as if that would somehow stop the pain.

As J.T. started to move away, Valdez reached out and grabbed his hand.

"Please. John Thomas. You end this pain for me, yes?"

J.T. could only imagine the pain the man was feeling. He had seen a lot of men gutshot and knew it was a slow, painful way to die. One he himself had sworn he would never go through if there was any way to end it. He knew Juan Valdez's request was a reasonable one, but he knew he couldn't do it. He couldn't bring himself to shoot a helpless man. There was another moan, louder this time.

"Please, my friend. I cannot stand the pain. For old times, you do this for Valdez. I beg of you."

Tossing Valdez's old gun aside, J.T. checked the Navy Colt he held in his hand. There was one bullet left. Cocking the hammer back, he placed the gun in the old man's hand. Valdez clutched it tightly, then looking up at the stars said, "You know, you should not have shot my horse last year. He was a damn good horse, John Thomas."

J.T. stood up. "I'm sorry about that, Juan. I was aiming for you, but my horse jumped."

Valdez managed a grin. "Too damn bad he didn't jump tonight. Thank you, my friend."

The hand holding the gun came up in one swift motion. Valdez put the barrel of the gun to his temple and pulled the trigger. His pain and suffering were over.

Taking the gun from the old bandit's hand, J.T. bade him a silent good-bye, then walked over to the campfire. With the toe of his boot, he rolled the body of the burnt bandit away and sat down. He was struck by the quietness of the place. Only the sound of the crackling fire could be heard.

Alone, sitting at a fire in the middle of the prairie with a sky full of stars above and dead men all around, J.T. Law slapped the dirt from a plate and spooned it full of beans from the half-spilled pot next to the fire. He would wait for dawn to go after the others.

THE BUZZARDS HAD already begun to circle in the sky above as J.T. rode away from the Baxter camp site. He left behind the bodies of six men still scattered about the ground and a single grave near a tree with a crude wooden cross. Hanging from that cross by a strip of leather was an ancient Colt .44. A monument of sorts to a legend who had made his mark upon the frontier and had now passed on. Behind the grave, carved deep into the tree, were the words JUAN VALDEZ—THE MAGNIFICENT BANDIT—R.I.P. A sign of respect from one man to another. John T. thought the old cutthroat would have liked it.

It didn't take him long to cut the trail of the four men who had fled during the night. They were heading southeast for Corpus Christi. J.T. figured that was where this thing would end, one way or the other. He had been dogging Nate Baxter for over three hundred miles now, and he was sure the man had had enough. He wasn't the type to keep running. Somewhere, sometime, he was going to stop and make a stand. J.T. felt certain that after last night a fight was coming and it would happen in the streets of Corpus Christi. He would have his answer soon enough. The town was only two hours away.

• • •

NATE BAXTER TOOK a drink, then reached over and slapped Tom on the side of the head. "Jesus! Will you quit cryin' 'bout that damn scratch on yer leg? It ain't nothin'."

The two *vaqueros* who had fled with the Baxters stood at the bar, drinking as they waited to see what Nate planned to do next.

"But it hurts, Nate. The bastard put a hole clean through my leg. It bled somethin' awful comin' here last night."

"Is it bleedin' now?"

"Well, no. But it still hurts."

Nate grunted, then laughed. "Hell, ya want to know what pain is, ask ol' Valdez. Poor bastard took two in the gut when he went down. Bet the old bastard died hard too. But at least yer still breathin'. That's more'n we can say for Charlie. You could be stretched out right next to him, so shut the hell up an let me think, will ya."

Tom poured himself a tall drink from the whiskey bottle and carefully leaned back in his chair. At least the whiskey helped take the edge off the pain. He had to admit Nate was right. At least he wasn't dead. Not like poor Charlie and those other fellas lying out there on the prairie. It had all happened so fast that if it wasn't for the hole in his leg, he'd swear it had all been a bad dream. All that screaming and yelling with guns going off everywhere, then that damn big buckskin horse trying to stomp him into the ground. He could still see Charlie jumping up with his rifle, firing at the bounty man one second, then the back of his brother's head flying off the next. He'd never forget seeing that, never. Downing the glass of whiskey, Tom poured himself another.

Nate stared down at the table. His hand slowly turned the glass that sat in front of him as he pondered their situation. This damn bounty hunter had sure made a mess of things. Their pa was dead. Coe could be as well for all they knew. Now Charlie was gone, leaving Nate with only Tom, who was already crying about his damn leg and would be shaky at best when it came to a gunfight. Losing Charlie was a major blow. At least with him and the two *vaqueros* they might have had a chance against J.T. Law. But Tom wasn't near the gunhand Charlie had been, and Nate had serious doubts if Tom had it in him for a stand-up gunfight.

He would like to think that in all that hell-raising and shooting in camp last night, somebody got lucky and put a slug or two in the bastard and he was lying out there somewhere wounded, or better yet, dead. But something told Nate he couldn't be that lucky. No, J.T. Law was still coming for them. He could feel it in his bones. The question now was, what did they do to stop him? Nate was tired of running. Corpus Christi seemed as good a place as any to put an end to it. Even as slow as he was with a gun and being hurt, Tom could still shoot. The two *vaqueros* would stand with them because of what Law had done to Valdez. And Nate figured himself to be a pretty good gunhand as well. That made it four against one. Not bad odds when you thought about it.

"Hey, Nate. When we leavin' here?" asked Tom.

"We ain't."

"What'd you say?"

"Ya heard me, boy. We ain't runnin' no more. We're gonna stand up to that damn bounty man right out there in the street."

Tom placed his whiskey glass on the table and stared across at his older brother. "You gone outta your mind, Nate. This fella done killed fourteen men before he even got on our trail. Hell, I lost count of how many he's killed since then. What the hell are you thinkin', Nate?"

"I figure we're four against one, that's what."

Tom began to laugh out loud as he flopped back in his chair. "An' Pa called you the smart one. Hell, Nate. The damn odds were eleven to one last night and look what he did to us. You said it yourself. We were damn lucky to get outta there alive last night. Now, all a sudden you think with the odds four to one we got some kinda chance. That's crazy, Nate, an' you know it."

Nate's face turned red with anger. He didn't like being laughed at. Leaning across the table, he raised his hand to slap Tom, but suddenly found himself staring down the barrel of his brother's .44.

"No, you don't, Nate. You ain't hittin' me no more, you hear? Now sit down or I swear to God I'll blow you down!"

Nate could see by the look in his brother's eyes that he meant exactly what he said. Maybe Tom had more sand than Nate gave him credit for.

"Easy with that thing, little brother. I didn't mean nothin'. Reckon that bounty man's got me where I can't think straight."

Tom eased the hammer down on the .44 and stood up.

"Well, you stay if you want, Nate. Me, I'm headin' for Mexico. Find me some little out-of-the-way village and disappear. Don't figure he'll keep lookin' for me forever. Give me my share of the money from those saddlebags an' I'll be on my way."

Nate realized that his brother was serious about leaving.

"Now wait a minute, boy. Ya can't just go runnin' off like that an' leave me to fight this fellow alone. We're family, dammit. An' family sticks together, don't they?"

Tom shook his head as he put his gun away.

"No, Nate. All we been doin' as a family lately is runnin' and dyin'. I've had enough. Give me my money. I'm leavin'."

"Well, hell, I've had enough too, Tom. That's why I said we'd end it here."

"You just don't get it, do you, Nate. We're no match for J.T. Law. The man's a goddamn professional. Hell, we ain't no good as gunfighters and you damn well know it."

Nate was growing weary of this conversation. He knew the real reason Tom was wanting to run. The man was a damn coward. That was something Nate couldn't stomach, even if it was his brother. Tom had raised hell like the rest of them, spent the money, had the women, and now that it was time to pay up, he was going to run away and hide, leaving Nate to deal with John Thomas Law. The more he thought about it, the madder he got. Well, by God, two could play that game.

"Tom, just give me a minute. One minute before ya head out, okay? I got us a plan. It won't matter who's the fastest gun either. Just sit down and hear me out. If ya still feel like leavin' afterwards, then fine. I'll dig out yer share an ya can get on that horse out there an' ride for Mexico with my blessin', okay? Just hear me out, that's all I'm askin'."

Even as a boy, Nate had always been able to talk his brothers into anything. Nothing had changed but their age. Tom sat down and listened as Nate went into the details of his plan. Tom and the two *vaqueros* would wait outside the saloon. When J.T. Law rode into town, they would step out into the street and challenge him. Nate would be waiting on the rooftop of the hotel a few doors down with his Winchester. He'd have the bounty man in his sights all the way. Once he made a move for his gun, Nate would fire. At the same time, Tom and the *vaqueros* would draw and fire to cover the sound of the rifle shot. That would put an end to J.T. Law and they could get on about their business. He ended the conversation by asking, "Well, what d'ya think, Tom?"

Tom had listened with interest to his brother's plan. He could have saved them both some time if he would have just come right out and said they were going to bushwhack the bounty man and be done with it. The only thing Tom didn't like about the whole thing was the part that put him, not Nate, on the street facing the gunfighter. What if something went wrong? The man was fast with those Colts of his. If Nate were even a second late, he and the two *vaqueros* were dead men.

"I don't know, Nate. What if—"

Nate cut him off before he could continue. He'd expected this show of hesitation from Tom, and he was ready for it. He knew that what he was going to say next would be the hook that would set the deal.

"But just think, Tom. Y'all be known as the man that outgunned J.T. Law. Hell, y'all be famous. Ain't nobody gonna mess with a fellow that took down that gunfighter. No, sir. Folks'll be buyin' ya drinks, and the women, hellfire, ya'll have to beat 'em off with a stick."

Nate saw Tom's face light up, and he knew he had him.

"Damn. Reckon that's right, Nate. Never thought of that. They'll all think I shot him. The man that outdrew J.T. Law. Now that'd be somethin' all right. Hell, even that damn Wyatt Earp up in Dodge wouldn't wanta mess with a man that had that reputation."

Nate kept laying it on. "That's right, little brother. So what d'ya say. Ya wanta go hide down in Mexico or do ya wanta be famous?"

Tom grabbed the bottle of whiskey and poured their glasses full.

"Here's to bein' famous, by God!"

Tom clicked glasses with his brother and smiled. This was going to work out just fine. Sitting back in his chair,

Nate thought of all the ways he was going to spend that money he had in the saddlebags next to his feet. Between the banks and the stage robberies, he figured they had close to $45,000 in those bags. Of course, with Coe and Charlie now gone, his share was a lot bigger than it had been. That put it at $22,500 each for him and Tom. That was just plain old simple math. But as he smiled and took a drink, he stared over the top of his glass at his brother and still wondered what he was going to do with $45,000.

TWELVE

IT WAS ALMOST noon when J.T. rode into Corpus Christi. The town seemed larger than he remembered, but then it had been three years since his last trip down this way. The streets were filled with people hurrying about their daily routines. Out in the bay, riverboats waited their turn to move into the docks to be loaded with cotton, while farther down, passengers disembarked from steamers while other passengers waited among stacks of luggage to board for the trip back up north.

It was a bustling town and like so many in Texas these days was growing by leaps and bounds. Although some parts of Texas were still recovering from the effects of the war, they were recovering quickly, and J.T. knew that meant the ever-advancing wonders of modern progress would not be far behind.

Weaving his way through the busy street, J.T. figured it was going to be hard to find the Baxters in a town this size. But that problem was quickly solved as J.T. looked up the street and saw Tom Baxter and two Mexican gunmen standing in front of a saloon. All three men stood with their thumbs hooked in the front of their gunbelts, watching him as he made his way toward them. There was no mistaking the look. J.T. had seen it countless times in other men. Tom Baxter and his friends were ready to get down to business, and J.T. wasn't going to disappoint them.

Stopping short of the saloon, J.T. tied Toby off at the hitch rail and took off his coat. Folding it over his saddle, he walked out into the middle of the street and began the walk. At the same time, the trio at the saloon moved off the walk and out into the street. The sudden realization of what was about to happen sent the townspeople scrambling for cover. In less than a minute, there were only four men left in the street.

As J.T. walked toward the trio his eyes kept searching the alleyways and rooftops for any sign of Nate Baxter. Coe had told him Nate was the gunhawk of the family, but he wasn't the one standing in the street. That meant he was using Tom as bait to keep J.T. occupied while he worked his way into position to take a shot at him. It was hardly an original idea. It was one that J.T. had dealt with on more than one occasion. But if that was the way they wanted to play this hand, then so be it.

The distance narrowed between the men. J.T. finally stopped, his hands hanging relaxed by his side. Tom Baxter and the two Mexicans closed to within thirty feet, then stopped. Baxter stayed in the middle of the street while the two *vaqueros* spread out to the left and right, then planted their feet, ready for the show to begin. J.T. still hadn't located Nate Baxter, but that wasn't going to stop him from doing what he had to do.

"Tom Baxter. I have a warrant for your arrest. The

charge is rape, robbery, and murder. Will you submit to this warrant?"

Tom Baxter laughed out loud. "You go to hell, bounty man! An' take your damn warrant with you."

J.T. had caught Tom's eyes looking up toward the roof of the hotel. It had only been a glance, but it was enough to tell J.T. where Nate should be lying in wait for the action to start. The location came as a surprise to him. He had watched that rooftop in particular because of its height, but then discounted it because of the three-foot hotel sign that went from corner to corner along the top of the building. It was a bad location for a shooter. He'd have to arise up to fire, exposing himself to gunfire from anyone in the street. Nate Baxter had fought in the war, and J.T. knew that any man with that kind of experience would never pick a spot like that. It was then that he realized what was going on here. Tom Baxter sure as hell thought his brother was up there. But the fact was, Nate Baxter wasn't behind that sign. He wasn't even on that roof. If anything, he was halfway to the Neches River by now. Of course, J.T. would never be able to convince Tom Baxter of that. But then, he didn't even want to try. He'd made a vow to kill every one of the Baxters, and he fully intended to do just that. Knowing that Nate wasn't around was going to make it just that much easier for him.

J.T. nodded toward the Mexican gunmen.

"*Vaqueros,* I have no interest in you. That business last night was just that, business. I buried Valdez this morning and left a marker for him. Now, I'll say this just once. You can step clear of this right now and walk away, or take your chances with young Baxter here. It's your decision. But I'd make it fast."

The two men looked at one another for a moment. The younger *vaquero* on the right was going to fight. J.T.

could see the fire in his eyes. The other one was much older, and was clearly considering whether all this was worth dying over. He looked at J.T.

"You say you place a marker for Juan?"

"*Sí, vaquero.* It's carved deep in a tree at the head of his grave."

The *vaquero* nodded his approval. Slowly raising his hands to his side, he began to back away from Tom Baxter, then moved to the boardwalk. He had dealt himself out of the game.

Tom Baxter didn't seem worried that the odds had suddenly changed, but then, why should he? He still thought Nate was on the roof with a rifle.

"You're a smooth talker, ain't you, bounty man." Raising his voice to make sure that people hiding behind their doors could hear him, he continued. "Well, you ain't talkin' your way outta this. We still got business."

"Don't want to talk my way outta it," said J.T. in almost a whispered tone. "I came here to kill you, not to take you back."

This statement appeared to worry Tom Baxter, and for a second J.T. saw a hint of fear come over his face, but then, as quickly as it had appeared, it was gone. What did he have to be afraid of? After all, he was going to be famous. With that thought still running through his mind, Tom Baxter went for his gun. The young *vaquero* did as well.

In the blink of an eye three shoots rang out and they all came from J.T. Law's .45. His first bullet had hit the *vaquero* squarely between the eyes before the young Mexican's gun even left his holster. Tom Baxter had been the beneficiary of two bullets to the heart, and was dead before he hit the ground, the look of total surprise still on his face. People began coming out of the buildings and alleyways to gather around and stare at the two dead men.

The sheriff and his deputies, who had suddenly appeared, came running up the street as well.

J.T. showed the sheriff the warrant and gave him the details about what had led to the shoot-out. Writing all the information down, the sheriff had J.T. sign it, then told his deputies to see that the bodies were moved to the undertaker's. His official duties completed, the sheriff bade the bounty man a good day and returned to his office.

Seeing the other *vaquero* standing near his horse, J.T. walked over to him.

"You made a wise decision, amigo."

"*Sí.* If only my young friend had been as wise."

"Do you know where Señor Nate Baxter has gone?"

The *vaquero* shook his head. "No, but I will tell you this. That gringo is *muy malo.* He uses his brother to buy him time to escape knowing that he will be killed. What kind of man does such a thing?"

"The same kind of man that shoots seven-year-old kids in the head."

The *vaquero* placed his foot in the stirrup and mounted his horse. "I think I go back to Mexico. But first I visit with Valdez for a little while." The man paused a moment, then said, "It was a good thing that you did for Juan. I thank you. I hope that you catch up to this Nate Baxter. He needs killing. Adios, amigo."

The two men waved to one another and as the *vaquero* rode away, J.T. wished him a safe journey. There were no hard feelings between them. As J.T. had said earlier, it was only business. This *vaquero* had known and understood that. The younger one had not lived long enough to learn the difference.

Three down and one to go, thought J.T. as he mounted Toby and started toward the livery stable. And the last one was the worst one of the bunch. Nate had already shown that he was capable of anything. As long as the man was roaming the countryside, no one was safe.

J.T. had learned long ago that the most valuable sources for information were whores and the owner of the livery stable. The whores usually knew why a man was in town and how long he'd be there, and the livery owner knew when he left and usually the direction he was headed. The owner had no trouble remembering Nate Baxter. Nate had bought the finest horse the man had, a roan gelding. It was a big horse, strong and built for speed. The owner even admitted to J.T. that he had asked twice the price for the horse, figuring Nate would try to haggle him down. But to his surprise, Nate had opened his saddlebags and come out with a fistful of money, paying the man's price without question. Then he had quickly saddled the horse and ridden out of the place as if the devil himself was after him. He had headed southwest when he left. J.T. thanked the man and rode out of Corpus Christi, leaving two men dead and with one name left on his list.

THIRTEEN

JOHN T. HAD come across two sets of tracks, either of which could have belonged to Nate Baxter. After checking them closely, he remembered the livery man saying the roan was a big horse, and so he chose to follow the set of tracks with the deeper imprint. He had been following those tracks all day, and now, as the light began to fade, he picked a spot along the banks of Aqua Dulce Creek to set up camp for the night. If Nate stayed true to the course he was now traveling, that would mean he was headed for the town of Concepcion. But why there, J.T. had no idea. He seriously doubted that Nate himself knew why. But J.T. could understand that. Nate Baxter was alone now. He'd lost his father and three brothers. There was a price on his head and a bounty hunter on his trail. That all made Nate a desperate man. And a desperate man was perhaps the most dangerous of all.

Finishing his supper, J.T. rolled himself a cigarette and lay back on his saddle, watching the flickering flames of the campfire. He found himself missing Coe Baxter's company. The boy had generally had something to talk about each night when they set up camp. He especially remembered their conversation about the young lady who had stolen his heart when he was the ripe old age of fourteen. Coe had gone on and on about her and how he hoped to see her again someday. But after all that had happened, he really doubted she would ever want to see his face again. He could only imagine the things she must have heard about him, including the tales of the bank robberies and murders they had carried out, and of that terrible day when they had robbed the stage. That was what had bothered Coe most of all. What self-respecting young woman would ever want to associate with someone who had been involved in a rape, let alone a bank robbery and murder? Just the mere mention of his name in the presence of her family would surely be enough to have her banished to her room forever.

The boy had asked J.T. if he had a girl. J.T. had told him that he didn't have time for such things. But of course that had been a lie. There were some things that the bounty man would not talk about, and that was one of them. Reaching into his vest pocket, he removed a gold watch attached to a gold chain. It had been a gift from someone special. Clicking it open, he stared at the picture inside. It was a picture of a young woman in her late teens, with long, light-colored hair that came down to her shoulders. The eyes were soft and penetrating, the face a work of art. She was a beautiful woman and her name was Sara Jane Woodall. The daughter of Walter Godfrey Woodall, one of the richest and most powerful men in Texas. And she had almost become his wife.

Things were so much different back then. His family had a ten-thousand-acre ranch, stocked with cattle and a line of the finest horses in the state. Although not as wealthy as the Woodalls, his mother and father were highly respected and always invited to all the best parties and social gatherings. That was where he'd met her. And as with young Coe, she had stolen away his heart the very first time he saw her. Sara's parents had not been concerned at first, thinking that it was only youthful infatuation and would pass. But they'd soon realized that was not the case. John Thomas had been eighteen at the time and Sara seventeen. She'd been rebellious and had refused to stop seeing him. In desperation, her parents had packed her off to Europe for a year, hoping that the long separation would put an end to their affair. But she'd written him practically every day and sworn that upon her return they would be married, with or without her father's blessing. They'd vowed that nothing would stop them.

They had not counted on a war when they had made that vow. The echo of the gunfire at Fort Sumter had hardly faded before Texas took up arms for the Southern cause and found itself involved in the War Between the States. To make matters worse, Sara's father had been a hard-core Union man who saw it not as war, but as treason, and hadn't minded speaking that fact to anyone who would listen. In the end, Sara had remained in Europe, while her family had been given a choice. Either leave Texas or end up decorating a tree from the end of a rope. The man who had given them that choice had been none other than Howard Thomas Law. J.T.'s father.

The watch he held in his hand had arrived only days before the war began. She had purchased it in Paris, where she had posed for the picture that was enclosed. He had carried it with him ever since. Once word of what had happened to her parents reached her, the letters had stopped. As had so many other things during that terrible time.

J.T.'s parents had died of the fever while J.T. was

fighting in Missouri. Their cattle and horses had all been stolen or requisitioned for the war effort. The ranch had been deserted, and soon fell into disrepair. By the time the war was over, J.T. returned to find that it had been sold for back taxes and bought up by Northern carpetbaggers. The man who had brokered the deal was the new Yankee Government's commissioner for Texas, Walter G. Woodall. Things had never been right between them since the war.

Rubbing his thumb over the picture, J.T. closed his eyes and could still remember the smell of her hair, the soft touch of her hands, and the warmth of her lips. It had been five years since he had last seen her. Things had not gone well at the meeting. There were still hard feelings on both sides. And his choice of professions had done little to improve his status in her family's eyes. Closing the watch, he made a silent vow that he would see her again when this thing was over.

Placing the watch back in his pocket, J.T. stretched out and settled in for a well-deserved sleep. He was determined that by sundown tomorrow, he would see Nate Baxter dead.

FOURTEEN

NATE BAXTER RUBBED at his tired and weary eyes. He had hardly had any sleep at all. The slightest noise was enough to bring him out of his blankets with gun in hand, halfway expecting to see John Thomas Law standing there with a gun pointed at his head, but finding instead only the darkness of the night and the silence of the prairie.

Sitting up and wrapping his blanket around him to ward of the night chill, he thought about how good a cup of hot coffee would taste right now. But he was running a cold camp, afraid that J.T. might be trying to somehow track him in the dark and that a fire would certainly lead him straight to his camp. That was the last thing Nate wanted right now. He'd already experienced the way J.T. Law entered a camp, and he had no desire to be a party to another such arrival.

He was disgusted with the whole state of affairs. Here he sat with $45,000 in cash, chilled to the bone, with no fire or even a damn cup of coffee to drink. And it was all because of one man. He'd like to think that Tom and the *vaqueros* had killed the sonofabitch, but the more he thought on it, the less likely it seemed. It was like the damn man had a pact with the devil. No matter what happened, he just kept coming. Like some damn demon from hell that killed everything in its path with those deadly Colt .45's of his. They had claimed his father and maybe Coe. Then Charlie, and more than likely brother Tom. There wasn't much, if anything, that scared Nate. But he had to admit, this J.T. Law had him as nervous as a whore in church. If only he could find some way to shake the man off his trail for just a few days, he could go back to his original plan.

That plan was a simple one. If he could lose the bounty man long enough to get back to Corpus Christi, he could get aboard one of the steamers heading back up north and disappear in one of those big cities. With the amount of money he was carrying, he could change his name and set himself up real nice. Maybe buy himself a saloon and become an honest-to-goodness businessman. J.T. Law would never find him up there. Nate was sure of that. The problem was getting out of Corpus Christi before the man could catch up to him. So far, Nate had not been very successful at getting that job done, managing only to stay ten or twelve hours ahead of him. The man at the livery had practically robbed him, selling Nate his horse at twice what the damn roan was worth. But he hadn't had time to argue the point. If he had, they would have found the bastard hanging inside his own livery. But as it was, he had barely made it out of town before he heard the echo of gunshots behind him. He'd only heard the echo of three, but from what he'd seen of J.T. Law, that would have been enough.

Nate had no idea where he was going or what he was going to do next. The town of Concepcion was still a day's ride, but he'd had no intention of going there, it had just worked out that way. The truth be known, Nate wasn't even thinking about direction when he raced that roan out of town. All he'd had on his mind was getting as far away from J.T. Law as possible. Now, here he sat waiting for dawn and with no more idea of what he was going to do than he had the day before. For now, all he could do was try and keep some distance between him and the bounty man until he could come up with an idea to get himself out of this fix. There was a way. He just had to figure it out, that was all.

J.T. WAS SADDLED and ready to ride at daybreak. He intended to find out if Nate had gotten his money's worth buying that big roan. There were few horses that could outlast Toby in the final stretch. His strength and stamina, matched with his speed, had proven instrumental in the capture of more than a few wanted men. J.T. felt today was going to be no different. If he had read the trail signs right, Nate Baxter was less than four hours ahead of him now. Prompting Toby with his spurs, he set out at a smooth but rapid pace. A pace that would continue until J.T. had Nate Baxter in rifle range.

"WHOA, YA LOOP-EARED bastard!" yelled Nate as he tightened the cinch too tight around the roan.

"Price I paid for ya, ya oughta be puttin' this damn saddle on yer own self."

Securing his bedroll and saddlebags. Nate hiked himself up and into the saddle. Taking a final look to the rear and seeing nothing but prairie, he walked the roan out of the camp site and started him at a leisurely pace. By his calculations, Nate figured he had a ten-to-twelve-hour lead on the bounty man. He saw no need to wear the horse out early. And besides, he needed to think. He still hadn't come up with a way to shake the man off his trail. He'd considered using the bushwhacking idea again. Waiting up in the rocks until Law drew within range, then trying to throw a couple of shots into him. But where Tom had been a poor hand with a six-gun, Nate was even worse with a rifle. If he didn't drop him with the first shot, J.T. Law would be on him like green on a frog. No, he couldn't risk it. Right now there was a good piece of distance between them and he wanted to keep it that way. But he still had plenty of time, and opportunity had a way of coming to Nate in the most unexpected ways. Nate Baxter wasn't done yet. Not by a long shot.

Only two hours after having broken camp, that opportunity presented itself in a most unexpected fashion. Nate came upon a covered wagon stuck up to the axle in mud on the banks of Gerogilis Creek. Farmers, it appeared, judging by the plow and other implements tied to the sides. A big fella who looked to be in his late thirties was out in front of the team of oxen, pulling on the leaders with all his might. To the side of the team, popping a whip with a certain amount of expertise, was a full-figured woman in a yellow dress and bonnet. She instantly caught Nate's eye. Yellow was his favorite color. Or at least it was now.

From what he could tell, all the pulling and the whip-popping was having little or no effect on the problem. Heading the roan down the slope toward the wagon, Nate caught sight of two blond-haired girls playing in the back of the wagon. One looked to be eight or nine years old. The other twelve or thirteen. This could be just the opportunity he'd been looking for. And with a damn good-looking woman tossed in for good measure.

Easing his horse into the swollen creek, Nate waded

across to the other side, giving the two girls a wink as he rode by. The couple, near exhaustion, had halted their efforts for the moment and watched the stranger as he approached.

"Look's like ya got yerself in a bad fix here, mister," said Nate, leaning on his saddlehorn and eyeing the front of the woman's dress. Working the whip had stirred the woman's blood, and the protruding nipples of her ample, firm breasts were clearly visible against the front of the tight-fitting material.

"It does appear so, friend," said the husband. "Ground seemed solid enough when I led them in. Not sure what happened. The wagon just started sinking when we got to this side. We'd certainly appreciate a hand if you wouldn't mind."

Nate was practically undressing the woman with his eyes. A fact that seemed to be totally lost on the husband, but one she was certainly aware of, and it made her nervous.

"Oh, no, Warren. No need to trouble this man with our problem. I'm sure he has other more important business than this. We shouldn't delay him. We'll do just fine."

Stepping down, Nate replied, "Oh, it's no trouble a'-tall, missy. Where y'all from anyway? I can't seem to place the talk."

"Ohio," said the man. "I'm Warren Brown, and this is my wife, Ellen. Those two giggle boxes behind you there are Mary and Tillie."

"Pleased to meet ya," said Nate. "Ohio, huh. Ya happen to fight in the war, Mr. Brown?"

"No, I was too young for it. But my two brothers did. They were with the 11th Ohio Volunteers under General McClellan himself. A true American hero."

"Yankee outfit, huh?"

Warren's eyebrows lifted slightly. "Why, of course.

An' you, sir. Were you a participant in the rebellion?"

Rebellion, my ass, thought Nate as he bit his lip before he answered.

"Nope. Had my hands full fightin' Comanches. Now, what d'ya say we get this wagon outta here and get y'all on yer way."

Nate and Warren moved to the front, each grabbing an ox by its rigging and pulling for all they were worth while Ellen went back to cracking her whip. After a few minutes of this, Nate stepped back and pointed to one of the rear wheels.

"Hey, Warren. Head on back there to that back wheel an' give her a push with a shoulder while I pull."

"Sure. That might work."

While Warren waded back toward the wheel. Nate's attention went back to the woman. *Damn, she's all woman, that's for sure.* Seeing Nate watching her again, Ellen turned away and gazed across the creek. That nervous feeling was stronger than ever.

When Warren reached the back wheel, he turned and put his shoulder against the corner of the wagon. When he looked up to tell Nate he was ready, he found the man standing at the edge of the bank with his gun drawn and pointed straight at him.

"What are you doing, mister? Don't point that thing at me."

"Since I ain't got that damn George McClellan here, reckon ya'll have to do, ya no-good Yankee bastard."

That said, Nate proceeded to shoot Mr. Warren Brown in the head. Ellen dropped her whip and came around the front of the wagon just in time to see her husband's body sink below the water. Throwing her hands up to her face, she screamed.

Nate reached out and jerked the bonnet from her head, revealing her raven-black hair. He could hear the children crying in the wagon and calling out to their mother, but he didn't care about any of that right now. He knocked her to the ground with his fist, and she landed hard, the blow nearly rendering her unconscious. Before she realized it, Nate was tearing and ripping at the front of her dress with his big hands. She tried to fight back, but that only brought another flurry of slaps and punches to the face that left her in a daze.

Ellen felt the material of her dress give way. When she opened her eyes, Nate was sitting on top of her with a knife in his hand. Grabbing the front of her undergarment, he pulled up on it and began to cut her clothes off. As her breasts pushed free, he pawed at them. She pleaded with him not to do this in front of the children. She wouldn't fight anymore. He could do whatever he wanted, only please take her into the woods, she begged. But it was far too late for that. Nate was like a man possessed.

Tossing his gunbelt aside, he pulled at the buttons on the front of his pants, then fell upon her naked body, driving himself into her over and over again, until finally, his animal urge had been satisfied. Panting, he sat up on his knees and smiled down at her.

"How d'ya like that damn rebellion, ya Yankee bitch?"

With tears streaming down her cheeks, her mouth bleeding, and her body racked by pain, she managed to utter, "Please. Don't kill us. Don't hurt my girls. Please."

Nate stood up. Fastening his pants and strapping on his gunbelt, he laughed. "Hell, lady. I ain't gonna kill ya. I need ya alive. But if ya don't do what I say, ya ain't never gonna see one of them girls alive again, ya hear? Now get up from there an' get yerself together. Ya look like a goddamn whore layin' there like that."

Forcing herself to rise and sit up, she saw her young daughters crying as they stared at her from the wagon. They had seen it all. Her hands shaking, Ellen tied the pieces of her torn and tattered dress together as best she could, then stood up. Wiping the tears from her eyes, she made her way to the wagon and held her daughters tight, trying to assure them that everything would be all right.

Nate yelled at her to get the girls out of the wagon and take them to the edge of the woods. She did as she was told. As they reached the edge of the woods, Ellen turned to see Nate tossing a burning oil rag into the wagon. Within minutes it became a raging inferno. Sitting with her girls clutched tightly to her, Ellen watched as everything they owned in the world went up in smoke. They had nothing left now, nothing but each other, and this man had threatened even that, and there was nothing she could do to stop him.

Nate had pulled some provisions from the wagon before setting it ablaze. Walking over to where the girls were, he tossed a bag in front of them.

"Ya wanta eat, ya better get to it now. That's all the food there is and when I pull out, I'm takin' it with me."

While the girls picked through the bag, Nate knelt down next to Ellen. Leaning over to within inches of her face, Nate said, "Ya know, durin' all the excitement, I done went an' forgot your name, darlin'. That ain't polite, seein' as how we're such real close friends now and all. What name was it that Yankee husband of yers called ya?"

The foul smell of his breath and the sight of his tobacco-stained teeth were about to make her sick. "Ellen. My name is Ellen."

Smiling, Nate reached over, grabbed her arm, and squeezing it tightly, began to pull her forward.

"Well, Ellen. Ya come on over here with me. We got us some business to talk over."

The pain was terrible as he tightened his grip. She wanted to scream, but didn't want to scare the children any more than they had been already. As she struggled to get to her feet, Nate kept pulling on her even tighter.

"Come on. Come on there. That's it."

When she was finally on her feet, Nate led her down to the creek. Pointing across to the other side, he asked. "What d'ya see out there, Ellen?"

She scanned the prairie on the opposite bank, then replied, "Nothing. I don't see anything."

"That's right, nothin'. But in a few hours there's gonna be a man ridin' a big buckskin comin' right over that rise there. An' he'll be headed to where we're standin' right now. When he gets here, I got somethin' I want ya to tell him. Ya understand?"

Ellen nodded.

"Ya gonna tell him that Nate Baxter has one of your girls with him and that if he—"

Ellen pulled away from the man, her face in a state of panic.

"No!" she yelled. "No. You're not taking one of my babies! They're just children, for God sakes. I'll do anything you want. But leave my girls alone. Please!"

Nate's hand came up suddenly, the back of it catching her square in the face and sending her sprawling to the ground.

"Ya don't do the tellin' round here, missy. Figured ya knew that by now. Maybe I need to get down there and give ya another hard ridin'. Seems ya forgot who's boss here."

He reached for the top button of his pants.

Ellen scurried to her feet. Wiping the blood from her nose, she grabbed his hand to stop him.

"No. You're right. I'm sorry. I just don't want either of my girls hurt. Surely you can understand that. Why does it have to be one of the girls? Why not me?"

" 'Cause that's not my plan. Ya tell this fella that if he

don't back off of me and give up this hunt, I'll kill the girl. An' he knows I'll do it. He's to give up trackin' me, ya hear? I see him comin' up on me the next three days, I'll cut the kid's throat right then an there. Ya tell him that."

Ellen's knees suddenly got weak. She felt she might faint any second. This was all too much for her. The very thought of one of her children alone with this animal. It was all she could do to stay on her feet.

"But what if he won't do as you say? That wouldn't be my fault or my daughter's. What do I do then?"

Nate's eyes went cold as a snake. "Well, lady, ya better pray ya can convince 'im. That's all I got to say. Let him know her blood'll be on his hands. Hell, if nothin' else, take them clothes off and offer 'im some of that. I don't care if ya pray 'im into stayin' or ya screw 'im into stayin', just as long as he ain't comin' after me no more. Now ya think ya can handle that?"

"Yes. I know what to do. But if he stays. What happens to my daughter?"

"I'll keep her with me for a couple days an' keep checkin' my backtrail. When I'm sure he's given it up, I'll leave her at the first town I come to. She won't be hurt none, if that's what's worryin' ya. I might kill a few of 'em once in a while, but I'd never done nothin' like I done to you to a young'un. I like mine a little bigger."

Nate reached out and cupped her breasts in his hands. She saw that look in his eyes. He wanted her again. Looking back toward the girls, who were eating, Ellen yelled to them.

"Mary. You and Tillie stay right there. Don't go off anywhere. I'll be back in a little while."

Turning back to Nate, she asked, "Could we go down the bank a little ways, then into the woods this time?"

Nate was all smiles. "Well, seein' as how yer bein' so

downright civil about it, I reckon I don't mind the walk."

They walked a short distance down the creek. Once Ellen was certain they were out of sight of the kids, she turned and silently began walking into the woods, undoing the ties on her dress as she went.

FIFTEEN

JOHN T. SAW the smoke in the distance. It was still a long ways off. His first thought had been Indians, but when the smoke continued to rise as one long pillar, he put that worry aside. Whatever it was, it was a fair-sized fire, and he was riding straight for it. He watched the smoke for almost an hour, all the time wondering what it could be. It wasn't a woods or prairie fire; the smoke would be white. This was dark, almost black smoke. The kind you saw when a home or a wagon burned. He didn't know of any ranches or farms out this way, but then, it had been a long time since he had been this far south.

Three hours later, Nate's trail was still as clear as a Colorado stream. The smoke had faded away, but J.T. had sighted in on a reference point in the general area. At the pace he was riding, he'd be there in less than an hour.

The smell of burnt wood grew stronger as he neared the creek. Cresting a small rise, he saw the creek and the remnants of a burnt-out wagon. A woman in a tattered yellow dress was standing knee-deep in the water going through what was left. From what J.T. could see, that couldn't be much.

As he started Toby down the slope, he heard a young voice cry out.

"Mama! Mama! There's a man coming."

A little blond girl came running from the woods and clung tightly to her mother, who had now moved to the bank and was watching him.

Reaching the other side of the creek, John T. touched the brim of his hat and nodded.

"Afternoon, ma'am. Appears you've had some bad trouble here."

J.T. saw that her face was battered and bruised and her dress hardly more than a tattered rag. There was no expression on her face and her eyes seemed distant, almost lifeless.

"You're John Thomas Law, I assume."

J.T. was momentarily taken aback. Removing his hat, he said, "I'm sorry ma'am. Have we met before?"

"No. My name is Ellen Brown. My family and I had the misfortune to meet the man that you're after."

Suddenly everything became clear to the bounty man. He should have known. The burnt-out wagon. The scared look on the face of the child. The torn dress and lifeless stare. All the work of that damn Nate Baxter.

The woman suddenly began to rock forward as if she were having a hard time standing. The next second she fainted dead away and crumpled to the ground. The little girl screamed out for her mother, then fell beside her calling for her to wake up. J.T. was out of the saddle and at her side within seconds. Pulling a kerchief from his vest pocket, he gave it to the girl and told her to wet it in the stream. The child grabbed it and ran for the water as fast as her little legs could carry her, then hurried back. Giving him the cloth, she asked, "My mama gonna die, mister?"

Dabbing the kerchief around Ellen's face, John T. shook his head. "No, honey. Your mother's just fainted, that's all. She'll be all right in a few minutes. Don't you worry none. Where's your father?"

The little girl turned on her heels and pointed to the creek. "In there. The other man shot him. Daddy went under the water and we never saw him again."

J.T. saw the tears running down her small cheeks as she spoke. He had noticed the bruises on the woman earlier, but now, close up, he saw the scratches on her arms and the bite marks around her neck. He didn't have to wonder how she'd gotten those. Nate Baxter had raped the woman. This little girl had seen her father shot dead. Had she also been witness to what had happened to her mother? John T. wasn't about to ask, but he hoped she hadn't.

After a few minutes, Ellen opened her eyes to see a kind face smiling down at her. It was a pleasant smile. The face had a roughness about it, but the eyes were caring eyes. Gentle eyes. "What happened?" she asked as she tried to sit up.

"You fainted."

"I'm sorry."

"No need to be. I figure I know what you been through. Any apologizing to be done, it should be me. Wish I could have got here sooner."

Sitting forward, Ellen wrapped her arms around her knees and rocked back and forth for a moment. "He didn't think you would be here this soon."

"Nate Baxter?"

"Yes. I never knew there were people like that in this world. He's . . . he's an animal, you know. He shot my Warren in cold blood. Just took out his gun and shot him right in front of the children. Then he . . . he. . . ."

J.T. gently placed his hand on her shoulder. "That's all right. No need in talkin' about that. I've been chasing the man a lot of miles. Him an' his brothers."

"My God. You mean there are more like him out here?"

J.T. shook his head. "Not anymore. Nate's the last one. I got one in jail and killed the other two. But Nate's the worst of the bunch. I guess there's no need in tellin' you that. Figure I'll have him in my sights soon enough."

Ellen's face went pale as she grabbed his arm. "No! You can't go after him. You have to stay here. I can't let you."

"Easy, Ellen. What are you talking about? He can't hurt you now."

"You don't understand. He's got my other daughter with him. She's thirteen, for Christ sake. If you go after him, he'll cut her throat. You can't go, Mr. Law. He'll do it. I saw it in his eyes. He'll kill her."

"Damn!" said J.T. Then quickly: "Sorry, ma'am. It's just that every time I think I have that sonofa. . . . He somehow manages to figure a way out. How long they been gone?"

"Two hours. Maybe a little longer. Why?"

He knew Ellen Brown wasn't going to like what he was about to say, but he had to make her understand that Nate Baxter had to be stopped, no matter what the cost.

"Ellen, I have to go after them and I have to go right now. I can't let Baxter get away again or he'll end up doing this to another family somewhere else. You know how terrible it was. Would you want it to happen to another woman and her family?"

She looked away and shook her head. "Of course not. But my daughter. My poor Mary with that . . . that animal. And us? What about us, Mr. Law? What do we do?"

J.T. walked over to Toby and removed a few items from a grub bag he had hanging from the saddlehorn. He then gave the bag to Ellen. With it came a frying pan, pot, and plates. Everything she would need to set up camp.

"Why, this is all of your food and things you'll need. I can't take this."

"Yes, you can, Ellen. I might have to be gone two, maybe three days. There's enough stuff there to carry you through till I get back with Mary."

"An' Nate Baxter?"

"I plan to send that bastard to hell."

He could see the concern in her face and the fear in her eyes. It was understandable. Her daughter's life was at stake. She would know no relief until she had the child safely in her arms. J.T. was going to do everything in his power to see that Ellen Brown got the chance to hold her daughter again.

Handing her one of his clean shirts and a pair of pants, he told her, "You feel free to do any cuttin' you want on those things to make 'em fit. Don't think that dress is gonna hold up much longer. These'll be warmer for you tonight anyway. I done put out a couple of blankets over there by your little girl. You gather up some wood an' get yourself a fire goin', I think you'll be all right here."

J.T. saw the tears welling up in her eyes. Putting a hand on her arm and tipping her face up to him, he said, "Ellen, I know tellin' you not to worry would be foolish. But I been at this business a long time. Nate Baxter won't even know I'm there till it's too late. But if I think Mary might be hurt, I'll back off and wait for another opportunity. Saving Mary is the most important thing, even if it means letting Baxter get away. I won't risk her life. I give you my word on that."

Unable to hold back the tears any longer, Ellen broke down. Wrapping her arms around his waist, she placed her head on his chest and wept uncontrollably. J.T. put his arms around her, then gently stroked her hair. She needed to do this. Needed to cry out the pain, the sense of loss and helplessness that had built up inside her. Finally, looking up at him, she said, "Please bring my Mary back to me, John Thomas."

"I will, Ellen, or I'll die trying."

Just before he rode away, J.T. reached down and handed Ellen a small bundle wrapped in a cloth. Reassuring her once again, he rode out in search of Nate Baxter and a frightened thirteen-year-old girl.

Watching him until he was out of sight, Ellen unwrapped the bundle. Inside she found a short-barrel Colt .45 and a box of ammunition.

SIXTEEN

ELLEN BROWN HAD said that Baxter wasn't expecting him to arrive at Gerogilis Creek for at least eight to ten hours. He had made it in three. That meant the killer wouldn't be watching for J.T. on his backtrail until sometime the following morning. That was exactly what John T. was counting on. By pushing Toby to the limit, he could overtake Nate by sundown. Once it was dark, he would make his move. If all went well, he should have a knife at Nate Baxter's throat by midnight. If he had already killed the girl or harmed her in any way, J.T. intended to tie the man to a tree and skin him alive, one piece at a time.

NATE HAD MARY on the saddle in front of him. She had already cried herself out in the first few miles, and since then had not said a word or made a sound. Nate had tried to talk to her as they rode along, but the girl remained silent. After a while, he stopped talking as well. Maybe it was best. He didn't need some kid whining and yapping all the time anyway. He had other things to think about. Like what kind of business he'd buy into once he got to the big city with all his money. By the time the sun began to set, Nate had already spent his loot ten times over in his mind, and owned everything from a saloon to a high-class whorehouse to a string of purebred racehorses.

Finding a suitable place to make camp near a creek, he bound Mary hand and foot and put her by a tree while he set about gathering wood. Carrying it back into camp, he paused a moment to reconsider whether or not he should start up a fire. What if he'd been wrong about the bounty man? What if Law hadn't been as far behind as Nate had figured? He gave the matter some thought, then laughed out loud. What the hell was he worrying about? If anything, the man might have reached Gerogilis Creek by sundown. If the woman was able to convince him to stay put, that was fine, but if she couldn't, and he was determined to follow, he'd have to wait for daylight to start tracking Nate again. And that creek was four hours away. By morning Nate would be long gone before the man was even in the saddle. Besides, Nate had run a cold camp the night before. He wasn't going to run another tonight. He saw no need to.

By the time he had the fire going, he rolled himself a cigarette from a tobacco pouch he'd found in the Brown wagon. He'd lost his somewhere along the way. But the real prize from the wagon had been a full jug of whiskey he'd found stored up under the wagon box. Warren Brown might not have known much about Texas sand-bottom creeks, or known to keep his mouth shut about Yankee generals in a Rebel state, but the man surely did have good taste when it came to drinking whiskey.

One hour and half a jug later, Nate was feeling fine. Not having anyone but himself to talk to around the fire, he staggered to where he had Mary hog-tied and carried the girl over and set her next to the fire.

"There now. Ain't that better?"

Mary remained silent. Her eyes fixed on the man who had killed her father and raped her mother. She was only thirteen, but the events of the last twelve hours had already changed her life forever. She had cried all she was going to cry, and she had lost her fear of this man as well. For the first time in her young life she experienced pure unadulterated hate. It wasn't fear that kept her silent, as Nate believed, but rather intense hatred.

"Ya gonna be a looker just like yer ma, Mary. Can see it already," said Nate, still trying to get her to talk to him.

"Aw, come on now, Mary. Ya can talk to yer ol' uncle Nate."

Calling himself Uncle made him laugh.

"Ya have a fellow back there in Ohio? Reckon ya did, bein' pretty as ya are an' with that corn-silk hair. I bet ya had them boys howlin' at the moon for a go at ya. Yes, sir. That right, Mary?"

Mary wouldn't even bother to look at him anymore. Instead, she focused on the carpet of stars above and thought of her mother, and of her little sister, Tillie. This did little to soothe Nate's attitude, which had gotten worse with each drink from the jug. He was determined the girl was going to talk to him before the night was over.

"What's a matter, Mary? Ya Yankee gals got yer nose up too high to talk to us poor ol' Southern trash? That it? I ain't good enough, huh? Hey! I'm talkin' to ya, goddammit! Ya answer me, ya hear?"

Mary totally ignored the man. Corking the jug and tossing it aside, Nate jumped up and in three steps was standing over her. He'd figured to scare her, but she didn't flinch a muscle or look his way. Kneeling down, he took her chin in a rough hand and jerked her head around to face him.

"Yer gonna talk to me, ya little Yankee bitch, or I'm gonna make ya wish ya'd never been born. Now ya say somethin', dammit!"

Mary looked the man straight in the eye, the things she had seen him do to her mother still fresh in her mind. She had vowed silence, but now, her hatred was too strong.

"You're a pig!" she shouted, then spat in Nate's face.

Nate went crazy. Wiping his face with the back of his hand, he grabbed Mary up by the front of her dress and threw her across the camp site. She landed on her back and rolled twice before coming to a stop against his saddle. The impact of the ground had nearly taken her breath away. Pain shot all through her body, but she refused to give him the satisfaction of crying out.

Stomping his way across to her side like some crazed bull, Nate rolled her onto her back, sat down astraddle of her, and stared down at her. His face was a mass of rage and his eyes were cold and mean-looking.

"Told yer ma I didn't go around pokin' young'uns, but I'm gonna make an exception in yer case, missy. If yer old enough to be spittin' in folks' faces, I reckon yer old enough to ride, by God."

Mary's worst fear was about to come to life, and it showed in her young eyes.

"Oh, scared now, are we?" Nate laughed. "Well, it's too damn late, ya little bitch. I'm gonna give ya some of what yer ma got today. That'll take the high-an'-mighty outta ya."

Nate reached down to her dress.

"You touch her an' I'll blow your goddamn head off!"

Nate's whole body went rigid. He slowly turned his head to the side. J.T. Law stood ten feet away with a double-barrel shotgun pointed straight at his head.

"Now, you get the hell off her, you sonofabitch!"

As Nate started to rise, J.T. stepped forward and swung the shotgun with all his might. The barrel caught Nate square in the mouth, busting out teeth and sending blood flying as he was knocked backward into the dirt. He wasn't moving.

Kneeling down next to Mary, J.T. pulled a bowie knife from his boot and cut the girl free. There were tears in her eyes as she asked, "Who . . . who are you?"

J.T. tried to reassure her with a smile as he undid the ropes from her feet. "It's all right, Mary. I saw your mother and little sister today. Made your mom a promise that I'd bring you back to her safe and sound. An' I keep my promises."

Mary reached out and clung to him tightly, crying and thanking him over and over again. J.T. was about to help her to her feet when she suddenly yelled, "Look out!"

John T. turned just in time. The club caught him along the neck and the shoulder, rather than the head, and sent him tumbling to the right. Nate charged at him again. J.T. grabbed for his shoulder gun, then remembered he had left it with Ellen.

Rolling out of the way as Nate brought the club straight down, J.T. drew his Peacemaker from its holster on his hip, but before he could bring it all the way up to fire, Nate backhanded with the club, knocking the gun out of J.T.'s hand, breaking three fingers in the process. Though the blinding pain of the broken fingers, John T. yelled out, "Run, Mary! Run! Run!"

The girl was on her feet and running for the trees as fast as she could. Nate didn't bother to look her way. She was no longer important. He'd find her again once he killed this bounty hunter.

Seeing the bent and deformed fingers on J.T.'s gun

hand, Nate bellowed out a laugh as he said, "Ya ain't all that much without that iron, are ya, J.T. Law? An' that's just the beginnin', ya sonofabitch. I'm gonna break every damn bone in yer body, time I'm done."

J.T. had rolled up on his knees. The Peacemaker lay only a few feet away, but he knew he would never have a chance to make the grab. He looked Nate in the eye.

"You talk a good game, Nate. Now let's see you get it done."

"Y'all never take me in, bounty man!" shouted Nate.

"Never had any such intention, Nate. I'm gonna do Texas a favor. I'm gonna kill you tonight."

Nate charged, swinging the club wildly left and right. J.T. dodged the first swing, but caught a glancing blow off his shoulder from the second, which sent him rolling again. Nate suddenly threw down the club and ran to where his saddle and bedroll were laid out. Grabbing up his gunbelt, he was shocked to see that his gun was gone. In a panic, he threw the blanket and his saddle aside in a desperate search, but the gun wasn't there.

"You were so damn busy goin' at the girl, you never heard me come in, Nate. I threw your gun away."

Nate turned to see J.T. holding the shotgun in his left hand, with the stock braced against his leg. Slowly rising to his feet, Nate knew the game was over. But he figured he had nothing to lose by trying to talk his way out of this.

"Looky, here, bounty man. I got forty-five thousand dollars in them saddlebags there. You can have it all if y'all just let me go. What d'ya say?"

"Hell, Nate, that ain't no deal. It'll all be mine in a minute anyway."

Nate's mind was moving a mile a minute, but he couldn't think of anything that he might say or do that would save him this time. Then suddenly he thought of the warrants.

"Hey, bounty man. Ya gotta take me in. Those warrants say dead or alive."

Throwing his hands high, Nate continued. "Well, I'm surrenderin', see! I ain't fightin' ya none. I got no gun!"

John T. lowered the shotgun.

"That's your damn problem!"

One barrel of the shotgun exploded, the double aught buckshot cutting Nate's legs out from under him, leaving one barely hanging on by a piece of shredded muscle.

"Oh, good God!" cried Nate. "Sweet Jesus!"

J.T. slowly walked toward the man who had spread so much pain, misery, and death across Texas for the last three weeks. From the bank killings to the Rangers in Nacogdoches. The family at the ranch whom J.T. had buried. Ellen, her husband, and her girls. They were all in his thoughts as he made that short walk to Nate Baxter's side. He hadn't been able to find it in himself to finish off Juan Valdez, but this somehow was much different. There was no sense of guilt or regret. There was nothing.

Writhing in pain, Nate looked up and shouted, "I'll see ya in hell, J.T. Law! Ya sonofabitch!"

"Reckon so, Nate. You be sure an' save me a seat in the front row."

With the twitch of a finger, J.T. fired the second barrel and blew the top of Nate Baxter's head off.

Sitting down next to the fire, he saw Mary peeking around from behind a tree and waved for the girl to join him. She glanced over toward Nate, then quickly turned away from the awful sight. Running to J.T.'s side, she sat down next to him and hugged him tight. They both sat quietly together for a while. J.T. was the first to speak.

"Reckon we better get you on back to your mother, don't you?"

She looked up into his smiling face and replied, "That would be wonderful." Then seeing his hand, she cried, "But you're hurt."

"It's nothing, Mary. Come on, let's go."

The reunion at Gerogilis Creek was one John T. would remember for a long time. Ellen set his broken fingers, fashioned a splint, and wrapped them for him. With Mary and her mother riding Nate's roan and Tillie aboard Toby, J.T. took them to Corpus Christi, putting them up in the finest hotel and giving Ellen the money to buy all new clothes for herself and the girls. Later, Ellen and John T. talked about what the Brown family would do next. Ellen had a sister who lived in Boston. She would take the girls there for the time being and try to start a new life. J.T. had his hand taken care of by a very reputable doctor who said there would be no lasting effects from the injury, which was good news for the bounty man.

Having spent a week in Corpus Christi, J.T. figured it was time for him to move on. He still had business in Austin. He was leaving on the same day that Ellen and the girls were to board the steamer for Boston. The farewell on the dock was a tearful one for the girls, with John T. looking a little misty-eyed himself. They all hugged and said their good-byes. Then Ellen and the girls headed up the gangplank. J.T. waited until they were halfway there, then called out for Mary to come back to the dock. As she walked up to him, he handed her a small, tightly wrapped package and told her to hide it and not show it to her mother until they were in Boston. It would be their little secret. She agreed and giving him a final kiss on the cheek, ran back to her mother's side.

Leaving the docks, J.T. headed for Austin. It was a long, hot trip, but his spirits rose when he saw the Manor

House Hotel sign in the distance. Tonight there would be a hot bath, good cigars, and fine whiskey. But first he had business with Abe Covington. There was the matter of the reward money, and then what to do with Coe Baxter.

Arriving at Ranger Headquarters, J.T. stepped down and removed a set of saddlebags. Tossing them over his shoulder, he knocked, then walked inside. Abe Covington looked up from his desk. A smile quickly appeared as he stood and moved around to the front of his desk to greet the bounty man.

"Well, if it ain't the hero himself. John T., it's damn good to see you. Sheriff in Corpus Christi sent me a wire about Nate Baxter like you asked. Hell of a job you done, J.T. Don't think the state of Texas is going to mind paying out the reward money for that bunch."

"Thanks, Abe." Pulling the bags from his shoulder, he handed then over to the Ranger.

"Nate had this with him when I caught up to him. There's twenty-five thousand dollars in there. Mostly from the banks, I'd imagine. Don't know what he done with the rest of it. Could've buried it, I guess. But that's all there is. I'll let you figure out who gets what."

Abe tossed the bags on his desk and pulled a bottle from the top drawer.

"Folks are still talkin' about you around here. Especially Billy Tyler. You sure enough saved their bacon in that canyon fight."

J.T. took the glass of whiskey offered by the Ranger and slumped down in a chair. Taking a long pull on the glass, he found that Abe's taste in bad whiskey hadn't changed since he'd been gone.

"It wasn't just me, Abe. Hadn't been for Coe Baxter and that damn eye of his with a rifle, that whole show could've went the other way. Where are y'all keeping the kid anyway?"

Abe took a drink before he answered.

"Boys were passing through Colfax on the way back here. The judge there found out they had Coe with 'em, he swore out a warrant on the spot and had it served before they got out of town. Since Colfax was the first bank they robbed, they had legal jurisdiction. He'd have to stand trial there. Billy and the other boys tried to argue the judge out of it, but he refused to drop it. The law was on his side. They didn't have any choice but to leave the boy in the custody of the sheriff there."

J.T. sat up in the chair, a look of concern on his face. "So they're holding him there for trial?"

"Well, they were. I talked to the boy myself. He told me your idea about the lawyers and all. Figured you'd wanta see him, so I got the attorney general's office to draft me up a transfer order signed by the governor, movin' him from Colfax to Austin for trial. Billy and Tom Overhalt rode up there yesterday to bring him back. Should be gettin' back here any time now."

That seem to ease J.T.'s concern, and he sat back in the chair with another glass of Abe's snakebite medicine. They spent the next hour talking about what all had happened since he'd been gone.

After their losses in the canyon fight, the Indians had lost faith in their leader and returned to the reservation back up in the Nations. Iron Hand, the young warrior chief who had aspired to be the terror of the plains in Texas, had been shot to death by a farmer when he rode up to beg for food. The sheriff in McKintosh County had sent a wire to Abe asking him to thank the bounty hunter for the decent burial he'd given the Craig family, who had been killed at their ranch by the Baxters. The sheriff also wished the bounty hunter luck in catching the bastards who had done it.

Finally, after three drinks, John T. said it was time for

him to go. He was hot, dirty, and tired. He told Abe he'd come by in the morning to fill out the paperwork. The men walked outside. Seeing two riders coming at a distance, Abe shaded his eyes against the sun to get a better look at them.

"That's Billy Tyler and Tom Overhalt. An' Coe Baxter ain't with 'em."

J.T. felt a knot forming in the pit of his stomach. If that damn judge wouldn't let the Rangers have the kid, he'd go get him himself.

The looks on the faces of the two men as they rode up told John T. they carried bad news.

"Where the hell is Coe Baxter. Mr. Tyler?" demanded Covington.

The Rangers looked at one another, then at J.T.

"They hung him," said Billy, the sadness clear in his voice.

J.T. felt his heart skip a beat at the words. The pain clear in his eyes, the hardened bounty hunter turned away and placed his head against his saddle.

"When was the trial? That judge was supposed to—"

"Wasn't no trial, Cap'in," said Overhalt, cutting Covington off. "They got word we was comin' with that release. Vigilantes broke in last night and pulled him out. They hung him out in front of the livery. Boy was still there when me and Billy rode in this mornin'. We cut him down an' saw to the burial arrangements 'fore we left. Sorry, Cap'in."

Billy cleared his throat, then looked at J.T.

"We're sorry, John T. It's our fault. We told ya we'd watch after him. Me and the boys had taken a likin' to him. Hell, he saved our asses out there. Goddammit, if we'd had any idea something like this was gonna happen, we'd have went up there, shot the hell outta the place, and brought the kid back ourselves."

J.T. took a minute to regain his composure, then turned to face Billy.

"No, wasn't your fault, kid. Wasn't anybody's fault. Every man makes choices in his life. Some good, some bad. The kid made a bad one. He rode with a bad bunch that played a rough game. Any man does that, he has to be ready to pay up when the bill comes due. When it happens, you mark him paid in full and move on."

The three Rangers watched in silence as John Thomas Law walked away, leading Toby toward the livery. There really wasn't anything left to say.

One week later, John T. was sitting in the hotel restaurant about to have supper when a boy from the desk brought him a telegram that had just arrived. John T. opened it.

It was from Boston and read:

JOHN THOMAS STOP RECEIVED PACKAGE STOP TOTAL SURPRISE STOP CAN NEVER THANK YOU ENOUGH STOP MONEY WILL ASSURE GIRLS NEW START AND BEST EDUCATION AVAILABLE STOP WE ALL SEND OUR LOVE AND 20,000 KISSES STOP GOD BLESS STOP ELLEN STOP

ONE

THE CONDUCTOR CAME through the door dressed in his black coat, crisp, starched white shirt, bowtie and square visor hat. Closing the door behind him, he started down the aisle announcing the next stop on the railroad line.

"Austin comin' up, folks. Austin. Twenty minutes."

John Thomas Law didn't bother to look up as the man passed; his eyes and thoughts were fixed on a handsomely engraved gold watch that he held open in his hand. There was a picture inside. It had been taken in Paris, France, at the same time the watch had been purchased. Opposite the picture the master engraver had written the words J.T. had read over and over countless times for the last ten years.

"To John Thomas with all my love, Sara."

As he read the words his eyes lingered on the picture of a young woman in her late teens. She had long, golden hair that flowed down beyond her shoulders. The eyes were soft, yet penetrating and the face, a thing of beauty. Her name was Sara Jane Woodall, and she wore an ivory brooch on her blouse depicting a willow tree flanked by two doves. The man knew the brooch well. It had belonged to his mother. Knowing of her son's love for the girl, she had given it to him to give to Sara.

J.T. Law had traveled four hundred miles to see her for the first time after ten long years. The last time he had seen her was before her parents had shipped her off to Paris. She had bought the watch and had the picture made there, then sent it to him as a sign of their love and wrote him faithfully every week. But then had come the Civil War: A war that had pitted brother against brother, fathers against sons and the steadfast southern Law family against the unionist Woodall family. She had remained in Paris throughout the war. Gradually the letters had stopped coming. Somehow the years had slipped away.

J.T. had returned home to a defended cause and a state that had been ravished by war, corrupt politicians and marauding Comanches. His family had lost everything: their money, the Bar L Ranch, cattle and land. It proved a loss his parents could not bear. His mother died just before John had come home and then his father had also succumbed. There was nothing left besides bitterness and resentment. J.T. had left Texas before Sara returned. Like everything else, when the letters stopped he figured he had lost her as well. For the next few years he traveled from place to place, a lost and often desperate man and not above resorting to crime to make his way.

A former guerrilla fighter and member of the notorious Bloody Bill Anderson command, he had perfected the art of horsemanship and proved to be a natural when it came to the use of firearms of any kind. At the age of twenty-one, his speed and accuracy with pistol or rifle had earned him the respect of every man in the command, especially two older members who had taken it upon themselves to watch over him during those bloody and violent years.

It was those same two comrades who later saved his bacon during a botched bank robbery in Kansas. The bank had been owned by the same big outfit back east that had literally stolen the Bar L after the war. J.T. hadn't looked at it as a real bank robbery—to him it was more like collecting on an unpaid balance. If there was any robbery done, it had been on the part of the bank. With his saddle-bags full of cash, a young J.T. had gotten himself boxed in a canyon by a posse fully intent on sending him to his maker.

Just when all seemed lost, the two old friends from the war came riding straight down that canyon firing colt .44's with both hands and giving the Rebel yell so loud it could be heard three miles down the canyon walls. Losing four of their comrades, the remainder of the posse had wasted no time getting out of there while the ex–guerilla fighters paused to reload. J.T.'s two saviors that day had been none other than Frank James and Cole Younger.

J.T. had rode with the James-Younger gang for two years. While most spent their ill-gotten gains, J.T. had saved his and when he was ready, bid the group good luck and farewell. No longer broke and destitute, he returned to Texas. The gold watch had traveled with him everywhere he went and the picture was a constant reminder of what could have been had it not been for the war.

In a trick of fate or justice, depending how one looks at such things, J.T. had planned to buy the family ranch back from the bank that held the paper and pay them with their own money. Money he and the James boys had been robbing from their banks all over Kansas and Missouri. Ironically, those same bank owners back east had lost so much money from the robberies that they had to fold, and the ranch was sold at auction. The new owner had split the property up and sold it off in sections until there was no longer a Bar L Ranch, but rather acres and acres of plowed fields and farmhouses.

It seemed that all his efforts had been for nothing. He didn't want any other ranch. He'd tried settling in but after all the years of war and riding with the most famous gang in the country, ranching seemed mighty boring. He began to drink and gamble a lot, until finally he had frittered away all his money. Nearly broke and with no place to call home, J.T. resorted to the only skill he knew—the gun. But he had vowed to Cole and Frank that his outlaw days were over and he had meant it.

It was during a poker game one night that a cowboy had mentioned that he had witnessed a gunfight up in Dodge on his last cattle drive. A fellow named Josh Randall had squared off with two tough hombres in the middle of the street. When the smoke cleared, the town was burying the two outlaws, and Randall was riding out with close to two thousand dollars in his saddlebags—bounty money offered for the two men, dead or alive.

That conversation had stayed with J.T., and the following morning he had walked into the sheriff's office, pulled a bunch of wanted posters off the wall, got himself a partner and set out on a new career. To outlaws, J.T. Law had become one of the most feared gunfighters and bounty hunters in the state of Texas. No less than nineteen men had been sent to their maker looking down the barrel of the bounty man's Colt .45 Peacemaker. Having been an outlaw himself, J.T. knew full well the tension and hardship of constantly being hunted. For that reason he always gave those he was after a choice—give it up or fight it out. Of the twenty-one men he had pursued, only two had submitted to arrest, preferring prison to a pine box and six feet of dirt.

His last job had been a long and hard one. He had tracked down the murderous Baxter Boys after they had gone on a rampage across Texas, killing, robbing and raping. He had looked at the watch and Sara's picture often during that chase and vowed to go and see her when it was over. Somehow in his own mind he had hoped for a respectful and joyous reunion, but that was not to be. After traveling four hundred miles he arrived at his former lover's home only to have the door slammed in his face by a butler who informed him that, "Miss Woodall has no desire to see, nor speak to you, now or at any other time."

Not quite the reception he had envisioned. He had walked away from the house feeling like a complete fool. But then, what could he expect? After all, ten years was a damn long time to get around to making a house call. As he turned to close the gate, he glanced up at one of the second-story windows of her home and saw the corner of the curtains move. She was watching him. He could feel her eyes on him. As he walked away, he couldn't help but think that somehow this was not over between them. If she didn't care, why was she watching him? It was enough for him to hold out hope that someday she would change her mind and at least meet with him. He was a stubborn man. He would be back.

J.T. was about to put his watch away when suddenly

the engineer hit the brakes. The passengers were thrown forward as sparks flew from the big wheels and the high-pitched scream of metal against metal carried through the car. J.T.'s head slammed against the seat in front of him. The gold watch flew out of his hand and slid out into the aisle. Women were screaming and men were cussing as they picked themselves up off the floor. They had been thrown around inside the car like rag dolls.

"What the damn hell is goin' on!" shouted a man in the rear of the car.

J.T., momentarily dazed, sat back in his seat and tried to clear his head. Glancing out into the aisle he saw the watch. As he reached down to retrieve it, a boot suddenly came down hard on his hand and a gruff, gravely voice barked, "Leave it be, mister an get yer ass back in that seat!"

Ignoring the pain to his hand, J.T. looked up into the barrel of a Colt .44 held by a big man with a bandanna covering half his face. Placing the barrel of the gun against J.T.'s forehead, the man slowly cocked the hammer back.

"What? Ya don't hear good, mister? I said put yer ass back in that seat—now!"

J.T. pulled his hand free of the man's boot and slowly sat up, taking note of the cold look he was receiving from the man with the hard brown eyes and an ugly scar across the bridge of his nose. Three more men with their faces covered entered the car as the train chugged to a stop. They were heavily armed and it was clear they meant business. Brown Eyes reached down and picked up the watch, admiring it for a moment. He nodded his approval and muttered from under the mask, "Thanks, friend. I needed a new watch." With that he moved on back to the rear of the passenger car.

There was the roar of a pistol as one of the new arrivals shot a hole in the roof of the car.

"All right, folks! Now that I got yer attention, y'all know what we're here for, so let's get to it. Unlimber them wallets and pokes, ya fellows—an ladies, y'all strip off that jewelry. We'll be takin' that along as well. Anybody looks like they're gonna give us a problem here, they'll get theirself shot on the spot. So get it up, folks. My boys'll be along to collect. Let's go!"

J.T. reached inside his frock coat for his wallet. As he did, his fingers lingered on the grips of the short-barrel Colt .45 he had concealed in a shoulder holster. For a second he calculated the odds. There were three men in front of him and Brown Eyes behind him. Taking down the three in front would require surprise, speed and accuracy. He knew he could handle that. The problem was the man behind him. Could he take the three in front and still make the turn to the rear and get off a shot before Brown Eyes put lead in him?

Influenced by the possible loss of his watch, he convinced himself that it was worth the risk and was about to make his move when his eyes fixed on the frightened face of a young mother across the aisle, clutching a baby in her arms. Looking down the length of the car he counted four more women with children seated between him and the outlaws. He quickly realized this was not the place for a gunfight with four train robbers. There would be plenty of lead flying in a confined space and it was a damn good bet that some of the women and kids could be hit before it was all over. As much as he wanted to take this bunch on and get his watch back, it wasn't worth the life one of these innocent women or children.

Removing his wallet from the inside pocket of his coat, he dropped it in to the open grain sack the men were using to collect their ill-gotten gains. Disgusted by the turn of events, J.T. stared out the window. For the first time since the train had been stopped he noticed four mounted outlaws with rifles positioned at various intervals along the length of the train. Looking out the window across the aisle he counted four more masked men that had taken up similar positions on that side. He was impressed. All had rifles and were well mounted. But what really drew his attention was the manner with which the outlaws set their horses. Ramrod straight, with shoulders back and rifles resting on the thigh, ready for immediate action should it become necessary.

A veteran himself, J.T. recognized a cavalryman when he saw one, and right now he knew he was looking at eight well-trained troopers. Shifting his attention back to the four men inside the train, he began to study their appearance and movements. It was a natural thing for a man in his profession. Once a bounty hunter took up a wanted man's trail he had to learn everything about the man he was after, no matter how small it might seem at the time. J.T. had learned over the years to memorize a description down to the last detail. Hair, eyes, build, any identifying scars, was he left-handed or right-handed, what kind of pistol or rifle did he carry, what color and kind of horse, anything special about the saddle, did it have initials or special design or ornaments. These were all part of the job, and a hunter needs to know what he's doing. More than a few in the profession had ended up swinging from a rope provided by local citizens for killing the wrong man.

He was equally impressed with the group in the train. They had tactically placed themselves at various locations within the car, which would allow for maximum observation while at the same time positioning themselves so that should someone challenge them, as he had considered earlier, they would not hit each other in an exchange of gunfire. This wasn't just another train robbery—it was a train robbery being carried out with perfect military precision.

As the men went about their business, J.T. began to catalog their appearance and movements. They might be the cock-of-the-walk and hold the upper-hand right now, but they were going to be seeing him again, and soon. They could count on that.

The train was suddenly shaken by a violent explosion. J.T. figured that was the express car safe being opened and he was right. The leader of the group looked at his watch and muttered, "Right on time. Hurry up, boys, we gotta be goin'."

J.T. glanced back behind him, searching for sign of Brown Eyes. He caught a glimpse of him just as the big man went out the back door. Again J.T. felt the temptation to go for his gun. Without the man behind him, he knew he could take the remaining three. But then what? More than likely, his actions would do no more than invite a hailstorm of bullets from the mounted men with the rifles. Common sense prevailed. His watch was gone. He was going to have to accept that for now. He would get it back, but this wasn't the time or place.

"We thank ya kind folks for your patience and cooperation. Now ya stay seated an we'll be on our way. In case ya didn't notice, we got boys on both sides of this train. Anybody goes stickin' his head out, they're libel to get it blowed clean off. Let's go, boys."

J.T. watched the men with loot mount and ride away. Then, with the same precision they had demonstrated during the robbery, the mounted riflemen began to withdraw. One man on each side of the train turned and rode out thirty yards, then turned back toward the train. Raising their rifles and keeping them pointed at the train, they remained in that position while each of their comrades peeled off and rode away. Once they were clear, the two rifleman booted their weapons and withdrew as well. It was a perfect rear-guard withdrawal.

The passenger car was alive with excited chatter as the train began to move again. The young woman across the aisle held her baby close and looking over at J.T. said, "Thank you, sir."

Surprised at her remark, he asked, "For what, ma'am?"

She allowed a slight smile to etch its way across her gentle face.

"I could see that watch meant a lot to you, and you appear to be a man that is accustomed to taking action in situations such as this. I could see it in your eyes—you were ready to fight those men. But you thought of me and my daughter and the other women and children on this train. I'm grateful to you for that, sir."

John T. found himself almost embarrassed. He had never been good at taking compliments, especially from women.

"I am sorry about your watch," she said.

"Oh, that's all right, ma'am. I'll be getting it back one of these days. You can count on that."

Flashing another smile, she replied, "I don't doubt that at all, sir."

The conductor reappeared once again. There was a trace of blood and a nasty-looking bruise along the left side of his forehead. He went about the car trying to restore some sense of calm by asking the passengers to make out a list of the valuables that they had lost so that it could be turned over to the proper authorities when they pulled into Austin. As he started to walk by J.T., the bounty man reached out and grabbed the conductor's arm.

"What about the express car?" he asked.

The conductor stared at the man in black for a moment,

clearly trying to put a name to this familiar face. Then it came to him.

"You're J.T. Law, aren't you? The gunfighter and bounty man, right?"

At the conductor's mention of the name, the passengers suddenly fell silent, their eyes directed to the pair. It was a name that most of them had heard or read about in the papers.

"You're him, ain't ya?" asked a man a few seats forward. "The man that tracked down and killed them murderin' Baxter brothers a few months ago."

"Thought I recognized you, Mr. Law," said the conductor. "To answer your question, they killed our express agent and the two guards with him. Got away with pert' near thirty-five thousand dollars. The company will be offering a reward for sure. You going after them Mister Law?"

"They took my gold pocket watch—what'd you think?"

The young conductor grinned from ear to ear as he looked at the staring faces of the passengers.

"Folks, you might not get your valuables back, but with Mister John Thomas Law here going after those boys, you can rest assured you're going to get some justice. I'd say their train robbing days are over—they just don't know it yet."

"Here! Here!" shouted someone as the others began to cheer and applaud for the man in black whom they now considered their own personal "terrible swift sword of justice." For a second time John T. felt his face go flush from embarrassment. He wanted to strangle the conductor, but politely nodded his thanks to those around him instead.

Thankfully, Austin wasn't that far away. Calm had been restored and everyone was traveling the final few miles in silence or quiet conversation. A few seats back, two young women were eyeing the tall man in black closely—admiring his broad shoulders, his well-groomed black hair and those haunting blue-green eyes that had sent a thrill though them when he had stood earlier and nodded in their direction. They guessed him to be in his mid-thirties's and they were right.

The train pulled slowly into the Austin depot. As John T. stood and walked by the two young women that had been admiring him from afar, he touched his fingers to the brim of his hat and smiled. The women blushed and he heard them giggling to each other as he stepped off the train. The depot became a veritable den of excitement as word of the train robbery quickly spread. Passengers couldn't wait to tell friends and family of their harrowing experience. With his bag in hand, J.T. left the depot and headed down the street for the Manor House, one of the finest hotels in Austin. Once he got a room and dropped off his bag he planned to visit his old friend, Abe Covington.